The Blood Girls

The Blood Girls

Méira Cook

THE OVERLOOK PRESS
Woodstock • New York

7ic

— m- 6/99 $ 24.00

First published in the United States in 1999 by
The Overlook Press,
Peter Mayer Publishers, Inc.
Lewis Hollow Road
Woodstock, New York 12498

Library of Congress Catalog-in-Publication Data

Cook, Méira, 1964–
The blood girls / Méira Cook
p. cm.
I. Title.
PR9199.3.C6398B58   1999   99-10236
813'.54—dc21
ISBN: 0-87951-945-2

*Originally published in Canada by Nunatak Fiction
for NeWest Publishers Ltd.*

Manufactured in the United States of America

1 3 5 7 9 8 6 4 2

to Mark, gentle reader
and for Dawne,
who taught me to read
gently

Secrets save me from dissolving.

—Anne Carson, *Plainwater*

The Blood Girl

S e v e n days before Easter Monday, in a small town north of Winnipeg, Manitoba, an eleven-year-old girl sitting in her classroom began to bleed from the palm of her left hand.

The first sign that anything was wrong was a red palm-print on absorbent paper. Donna Desjardins sat during art class, drawing a picture of the Madonna and Child and colour-ing it with wax crayons when her left hand began to bleed from the palm. Her teacher escorted the young girl to the sickroom but when the school nurse washed the blood away, no wound was visible. As a precautionary measure the nurse washed the hand with disinfectant, bound it in surgical gauze and returned Donna to her classroom. Within two hours Donna's right palm began to bleed.

In fact, before she began to bleed, inexplicably, from the palm of her left hand, Donna was a healthy child. Her family had no history of prolonged bleeding or psychological disorder. Although sensitive and imaginative, she was assessed as emo-tionally stable. As one of three children, she lived in a crowded but, to all appearances, happy home. At first, doctors at the rural hospital in Annex reported that even when they examined her palms under magnification they could discern nothing but unbroken skin. Soon after, however, a small blister the size of a dime, the kind that grows over a burn, blossomed on the centre of each palm.

The small town of Annex where Donna and her family live, in the rural municipality of Daglunes, lies two hours north of Winnipeg, along Highway 8. The bleeding occurred in the week before Easter Monday during the first of the spring freezes. That was the year of the long drawn-out thaw, with snow falling well into May. People remember that time for the inclement weather and the hordes of reporters and television crews who swooped in and set up makeshift interviews and press conferences, demanding information from medical staff and clergy alike, and speculating endlessly on the symptoms of the Blood Girl, as Donna came to be known.

On the second day, Donna began to bleed from the sole of her left foot, a day later from the right foot, and the next day blood ran from her side. Five small blisters appeared above her diaphragm and it was from these that the blood flowed in an erratic but unimpeded trickle. Three days before Easter Monday, an uneven scattering of blood droplets appeared about the crown of her head. On Good Friday, the fifth day of her experience, Donna bled from all sites simultaneously. She felt extreme pain and towards evening lost consciousness. When she woke hours later, all her wounds had closed. No scars or marks could be found on her body, and the child appeared to be well-rested and in no pain. Since that day, Donna has experienced no further bleeding.

The reporters had much with which to concern themselves. For a short week in late April, the small town of Annex became the object of tense expectation and an entire country's disbelieving scrutiny. Her mother allowed no interviews and the doctors refused photographers entry into the child's hospital room. Nevertheless, an illicit photograph does exist, testament to the ingenuity of the Press, and it was published—to great controversy, as it happened—in the pages of the early edition of a National newspaper, only to be retracted from afternoon editions following a court order. The photograph is imprecise and blurred, but its subject gazes out at the viewer from between widely spaced, startled eyes. Indeed, the extraordinary impact of the newspaper photograph can be traced to the disparity between the camera's imprecision (occasioned, perhaps, by a photographer's trembling hands?) and the uncanny clarity of the child's gaze. That and the dark blood clotting her hair.

None of the doctors who examined her, first at Annex, and later Winnipeg, described her as a hysterical personality. Although approaching adolescence, she had not yet begun to menstruate, and her body was that of a child's—in all particulars she was undeveloped and prepubescent. Despite the painfulness of her situation, she seemed a stable and contented young girl not prone to neurosis. Her family regularly attended Our Lady of Perpetual Mercy and All Saint's Catholic Church, and Donna herself was said to identify strongly with Christ's life and sufferings on the cross. Nevertheless, and given her extreme youthfulness, there seemed no reason to doubt her, Donna Desjardins denied any knowledge of the phenomenon of stigmata before she herself experienced it.

Gentle Reader,

Not many people can say they've lived in the same house all their life. No, the word home, through all its transformations, through all my journeyings, has never meant anything less for me than a house with green shutters and an open-faced look. In my imagination the front door is always ajar, the Lalique vase my mother brought with her is full of St. Joseph's lilies trumpeting through the noon, and the house itself is flooded with light. At moments like this I don't think I have a story to tell. Perhaps at most the shape we Rhutabagas have made on the map of the world in our separate journeys. Grandpa worrying his way through the barley fields, through mustard and rye and the sweet bye and bye of flax, his mouth turning in on a drawstring so that the farther north he travelled the more he clipped off his words at the root. Then my father built this house, squared off the fields with chicken wire and ploughed them into thick corduroy furrows. What was it father used to say to my brothers when they left, one by one, to work

in the cities? *No matter where you are, you are here.* My father was
a man of some discernment, as fond of a well-turned phrase
as he was of a nicely shod foot. He, at any rate, is still here, a
benevolent spirit, he hovers above the threshold blowing smoke
into these dim rooms from the ghosts of the cigars he was so
fond of.

From the kitchen I can smell butter cooking, a thick yellow
heat, the sound of a wooden spoon knocking against the side
of a bowl. My companion, Regina, is busy today, a somewhat
more corporeal *genu loci,* she leans against the stove, stirring
and tasting, catering to her careless eleven o'clock hunger. She
and I talk often of nature because it is something about which
she is vehement and I am skeptical. Nature, she says, has perfect balance. For me, this is not something that has practical
application. Although I was raised in the country, as mamma
would have said, I have always known, yes, deeply and suc-
cinctly, that what leads to death is only information. And God
being absent in all this is not helpful, not kind.

I have always liked books more than people, although I have
never trusted either. When I was young the world began at the
edge of the page and real life was something that happened
after father ordered me to shut that darned book, girl, and do
your chores. My brothers called me a bookworm and worse but

their voices dimmed between the rustling of pages as I fell like Alice into language, my skirt whirling above my head. I read my way through a British girlhood of stately homes and bone china, of fox-hunts and buttered toast and suitors who looked as well in their riding habits as in formal dress. Outside, the wind rubbed maple leaves to rag, the prairie sun crawled across my legs as I hung between earth and sky on the hammock father strung between two hitching posts, and read about ruined abbeys and rolling hills and hedges thick with something called larkspur. Behind my oblivious head flowering bushes—not larkspur, not hawthorn, not yew. They were not in any of my books.

Where was I? My thoughts are so disordered these days. Aah yes, nature. Well it is useful, for one thing, as a system of correspondence, the ground against which to measure what is truly human. Regina, for instance, in all her human splendour of jut and flaw, Regina who has just brought me a cup of lemon tea and an oatmeal cookie. (One is very sour, the other very sweet. Neither is just right.) For me, Regina, with her dense flesh, is the giant rhizome that grows beneath the ground all summer until, oh—August, when she gains great pumpkin inches as you watch. What I want to say, what I keep distracting myself from saying, is the fact of her, Regina, in my kitchen, a tired woman with black fingerprints beneath her

eyes, her skin thin and chaffed with sleeplessness. Her movements are filtered, she puts a clenched fist to the small of her
back, stretches in that bone-weary, shoulder-heavy, running on
oilrags and bottom of the grease-barrel way. There is something
in her languor, her hopelessness even, that inclines to the
horizontal plane. I have known Regina all my life and, as is
the way with such friendships, seem at this moment not to
have known her at all. Where does the loss of love begin? What
is the opposite of passion? Patience, passivity, fish-fingers, the
Sears catalogue, white socks, the bingo. The way she pushes the
vacuum cleaner about these days! A slow, deliberate oblation,
bend and slide, bend and slide.

I watch her, half in admiration. No, more than half. She, at
any rate, has perfected the practice of living as an adventure
of the body. My own body these days feels slack, loose-boned,
stuffed with sand. Not merely old but blunt. I thought writing
this memoir would hone me, draw me tight and taut, set the
blood to flight just below the surface. And who knows, it might
still happen. These days fiction is no less credulous than auto-
biography.

I am sorting my life, keeping it at bay, writing down dates and
times, shrinking chaos to the size of a trim white page. Lists
promise order, a life lived with decorum and propriety. And still

time to fill the vases with flowers, still time to read the newspapers—both the Annex weekly and the city daily—time to
smooth them down, fold them up, and set them out back for
the recycle bin. And yes, it's hard writing now after all these
years. Not just metaphysically either, my hands taciturn with
arthritis, and my eyesight equivocal. I manage well enough
with the help of the magnifying glass Daniel Halpern brought
me, along with his folders of transcripts, notes, interviews,
and lists. As for the pain in my joints, I take two of what I call
the bumble-bee pills that Ginny prescribed, and which come
in their suggestive yellow and brown gelatin capsules from
Turkle's Pharmacy in town.

Virginie Waters, who is the town doctor, lives in the small log
cabin that father built for the labourers over the harvest month.
Since then I've had Geisler knock down a few partitions, build
cupboards and install electric heating panels on the walls, so
that with a lick of paint here and a couple of my own rag-rugs
there, the place is warm and hospitable even during our hard,
crackling winters. This last winter, for instance, I hardly saw her
except when she sat reading in her window late at night, the
lamp throwing alluvial shadows against her neck. Like the rest
of us, she has had a hard time this year, a moth-woman caught
behind glass. The mystery that gripped our town is still saline in
her veins. This evening she came in soaked to the bone after

one of our curt spring showers. This is not the kind of town where people carry umbrellas.

Regina has just come, ostensibly to take away my empty cup, but I suspect her of an encroaching and fraudulent curiosity. She will not, for instance, take my arthritis for granted, but fusses over my hands, rubbing in lotion, massaging my fingers. And while it is true that I have begun to wear gloves in all seasons (even typing these notes on the old Smith and Wesson manual I used when I began my book on the true North), my motives are strictly medicinal. I have read, for instance, in one of papa's old *Reader's Digest* magazines I think, that heat is emolutive. Besides, I am trying to slow down, to enjoy the slight resistance of my leather gloves as I smooth them, the perishable taste of tea.

Recently I began to re-read all the highly coloured romances and poetry of my youth. But there is a difference, this time I am a gentle reader. When I was young I would tear the inside out of a book as if it were a loaf of bread hot from the oven. Jaw locked, knuckles white, I would have wrested sense from those densely printed pages by force, if need be. Now that I am older I read slowly, luxuriously, as if time alone can distill meaning from the page, each word a mouthful of brandy to warm against the palate. The phrase *gentle reader* pleases me because of how it was used in the last century. As if it were possible, now as then, to imagine a reader's ear pressed up against the tilted page. Today the book in my hands flutters as if to invite the tribute of a head drooped gently above its pages.

I first began to write after I lost everything else—youth, ease of mind and body, even gravity. Now I renew, periodically, my dues. I have asked Regina to turn on the radio. Something by Brahms filters through these dim rooms, the strings following each other in tightly interlocking sequence like silver links of chainmail or the scales on a freshly caught fish. Along the way I began to realize that we are all connected, not just to one another but to the elements, the mineral deposits of time. Forgive these fanciful digressions, I am an old woman in a dry season, trying with words to approach my psychosomatic death.

Take Regina, for example. I first knew Regina when we were girls together; Mina Isaacs, the Hukic girls and me, Molly Rhutabaga, in our brief, our frantic spring. In reality, Regina was not one of the Hukic girls, she was an Arnott from the valley but she came to live with the Hukics after her mother died. There was some blood connection, I believe, between Alisha Hukic and Regina's father. Certainly she lived in the Hukic farmhouse on sufferance, but later, when Alisha Hukic

got too sick to remain on the farm and took up residence in the
Care Home under the ministrations of old Doc lsaacs, Regina
began to take on a certain substance in that household. I
remember, she cut her hair from "sit on it" as my mother used
to say, to watch out ears you're comin' through. And quite
soon after that she began to grow into her body, her bones
sinking deeper into flesh like honey, eased, although if you
didn't know any better, and few did, all you would notice was
that she was putting on weight.

She was unfailingly soft-hearted, was famous for scraping
dead animals off the highway, giving them a proper burial. I
came across her once fashioning a memorial cross from two
twigs. Her mouth was pursed with absorption, the point of her
tongue just visible. But her eyes when she looked up were
blank. Something was absent, missing, nothing there when you
looked up after the shadow had passed. People were always
asking her, where's your accent from? As if it were separate
from her. That was the impression she gave, as if she were an
unlikely collection of spare arms and legs and flying hair, held
together by nothing so much as centrifugal force about the
fulcrum of a migrant heart. And you couldn't blame a body for
sounding foolish when they were in the process of being fooled,
could you?

Mina, Molly, and Regina, we were girls together, our hearts stirring for the birds that left, flew south. Mina and I married early because that was expected of young girls in those days. I married Robert Dunning because he asked father for my hand with such uneasiness that I knew he expected to be refused. I did not want to encourage such pessimism so I married him. As for my father, he drew deeply on his cigar. Then, with the smoke billowing dramatically from his mouth he roared, yes, yes, take her hand, take the rest of her, just don't bring her back! For her part my mother said, if you love him, go with him. I did and then I no longer loved him and so I left again. Besides, I missed this house.

The Brahms concerto is coming to an end, the cellos weeping, the violinist sobbing into the crook of her elbow. I remember the weight of his long blond jawbone and the plates of his shoulder blades as he bent over the farm accounts, agitated, then resettling. As I looked at him wings, the pages of a book, years, seemed to rush through the air. When I left I took nothing with me but my books, the name I was born with, the clothes on my back. Sometimes I think he just distracted me from the loneliness of living in one body. I remember sitting at a window, the trees in the avenues still bruised by the spring. They held the world in their branches, faithfully, treacherously. There is a lesson to be learned from this. I have become a woman who sits at a window, who watches.

And today, after all this time, here in this place, it is past
spring. After the first here-today-gone-tomorrow days, the town
finally tossed in its lot with the trees and exhaled discrete green
breaths. One day it was nearly-nearly, and the next summer
was already past. Regina came to "do" for me after her boarder
reported a strange smell and the sound of hair growing in the
crawl space below her kitchen. Later we found out that it was
only the bodies of gophers tenderly stacked above ground, waiting for the first spring thaw to be buried. But after our recent
scandal it has been generally agreed by everybody, from
Virginie to our Priest, Father Ricci, that Regina Arnott requires
discreet supervision. Besides, she is an inoffensive guest and
a storyteller of some fortitude. What is more, she understands,
as I do, the way our lives intersect with cutlery and garden
salads and the weather channel. This cup with its glaze of lapis
lazuli, for instance, placed in the world exactly so, to hold down
a corner of the day.

It is perhaps time to speak of Halpern. Daniel Halpern came
to our town as a journalist after the first blood miracle. It was
his job to be skeptical, a task undeflected by his inclination to
the most craven forms of adoration. Shortly after we became
friends he told me that he had always longed to live out a life
of stone, a noncommittal life. We were drinking sherry in the
living room, I invited him to dinner because Father Ricci had

hinted that he was several cuts above the ordinary, that he had read Aquinas, that he was, in short, deserving of my gentle and diffuse goodfellowship. I took up the Father's half serious, mostly not, suggestion with enthusiasm, more to lighten my own oppression than to allay his. Life in this town often has the appearance of boredom. I was anxious to learn more about this oddly haunted stranger, with his hunched gait and his carefully curtailed smile. It was in the living room, as I say, while sipping sherry, that he confided to me his petrified longings. I grew up in this country you know, he said, but it's not like coming home again.

It had been an odd day for me too, a slump in the middle, lethargic about the edges. Now, with the lamps lit, the shadows were geometric in their clarity. A shadow from papa's silver clock threw itself over his face and throat, drawing his left side towards darkness. I felt exasperation and then relief, the latter rising to the surface like the colours in an oil slick. He helped himself to cold salmon and began to describe what he called his lamentable susceptibility to love. Because this inclination and his resistance to it were equally strong, I knew we would become intimates. By the time we were eating papaya with port off mamma's coral dessert plates, and the candles had thickened about their wicks, our friendship had spanned decades.

It may surprise you to learn that we hardly spoke of the blood girl, the story he had come north to rout, and for whose rigours of spectacle and satire he was so clearly ill-suited. He had read my book, and so we talked of the muscular rivers of the North. I remember he said something like, *you have to go to the North to imagine the North*. Perhaps I have it a little wrong, but it caught my attention. There was something elegiac about him, one felt that in him the soul's pale stone was newly quarried. That he was in pain of some kind was clear, but whether it was metaphysical or the other kind I did not try to guess. He had about him a melancholy that so exactly suited my own need in a companion that I hardly dared inquire as to its cause. Not precisely sadness but a wax imprint of sadness, like a footprint in wet sand.

I don't mean to be evasive. It's true that we spoke once, not so much of Donna Desjardins as of his incredulity in the face of her wounds. At first Halpern snorted through his nose as if imitating a hard-assed reporter. Either it's an elaborate hoax, he told me, flinging up his hands to announce his unwillingness to take part in such messiness, or it's a medical condition that hasn't been discovered yet. I watched the fire in the small hearth imprint itself on the surrounding shadows. Nothing is inexplicable anymore, he continued, just difficult to name. There was a note of pleading in his voice but I paid no atten-

tion. What is it that makes you so uneasy, Halpern? I asked.
But he had already drawn silence fastidiously about him. There
is something about excess that he can't forgive, a lack of
restraint he finds impossible to approve. Come on boy, I teased,
get off your high Protestant rocking-horse!

He visited often after that and we embarked on a friendship of
almost perfect inequality, he was the boy with kind hands to rub
my mind to life. The world to me is, has always been, tactile, a
surface inviting the hand's imprint. He came to me after it was
all over, his arms piled high with folders and files. Here, he said,
make of it what you will. Then he left. When I was twenty, I
thought the world was effortless, my place in it assured. Now I
am hesitant, tentative, without wonder. I am the woman to
whom others come with their stories. I am a woman who sits at
a window and watches, then closes her eyes.

What follows, gentle reader, is a story cobbled together from
journal entries, transcripts, memory, interviews, coincidence,
newspaper articles, desire, imagination, correspondence, and
invective. Above all, any resemblance to characters living or
dead is both impure and unintentional. Imagine you are somewhere dark shot through with a single arrow of light. Someone
has put this book into your hands, it is a project in Braille. Put
your fingertips to the page. There. There. . . .

The Blood Girl

T h r e e things happened in the week before Daniel Halpern
set out for Annex to investigate the strange stories of blood
miracles. Almost concurrently, his vacation, which he had for
the longest time evaded, fell emphatically and, because of fed-
eral cutbacks over the last year, unavoidably due. And the
monthly magazine for which he sometimes provided the odd
pseudonymous piece asked him to write an investigative article
on what its feature editor with a well-bred grimace called,
"that blood and guts thing down in Annex." Although he had
long since trained himself to pass charitably over his own
motives, although he was careful not to anatomize the precarious narrative that others called fate, Halpern was aware of a
relief that began in his mouth as the taste of iron filings. Later,
when he had packed his overnight bag, when the hard metal
nose of his Chevy was nudging the fields of sky and snow along
Highway 8, he was suddenly, sourly, grateful for the contin-
gencies that obliged him to fill up his time with other people's
tart urgencies.

The third thing that happened was at once astonishing and commonplace. A routine physical exam he had taken to comply with the newspaper's annual insurance program came back with a number of disorderly red marks and circles that, in turn, prompted an "important but not urgent" call from his doctor. More tests were needed and Halpern, whose besetting sin was impatience, was required to submit his body to all manner of procedures. At any rate, he was not dying. "Not yet," said Dr. Hawkins looking down at his own spade-shaped hands with their blindworm fingers, "but it'll have to come out."

Halpern realized he had a crooked face. One side was earthbound, practical, the other seemed to want to fly off its own axis. This accounted for his characteristic expression, a kind of devout reticence composed in part of a mouth crumpled by its own perplexity and eyebrows as mobile and black as Spanish cedillas. At times, especially in moments of intensity, he resembled an early El Greco mystic, one of those desultory saints caught in a window and passionately trying to distill from the body's matte flesh the pale transparency of a soul. What added to this impression was a habit he had when roused of throwing up his hands, palms outwards. His fingertips were pointed, his hands very faintly triangular.

Daniel Halpern paused at his reflection flung peremptorily against the mirror of the men's room at the doctor's office, then stepped backwards and out of view, waving his hands impatiently through air to dry them. It was not a moment he would then or afterwards remember, since Halpern set no store by the body or any of its hasty alliances. He was a man addicted to periodicity, to lists, a man who no longer tried to make distinctions between the ordinary and the visionary, and this left him less with a sense of wet-lashed wonder than with a weary susceptibility to what he would nevertheless have a hard time writing sober on the page, the *miraculous*. His colleagues at the *Winnipeg Herald* were altogether bolder, more excitable, more, if it must be admitted, *successful,* than he was in their pursuit of those sly etceteras that convert newsprint into moveable assets.

A watery sunset scrolled itself across the prairie sky as Halpern walked home. The first woman who ever loved him back—a woman with a perfect columella and immaculate posture—had accused him of reversing into the future, improvising for dear life. And of what do you have to be so proud, so *fruitless?* she had asked once, an inexact translation in her transgressive English. *Godi la vita anche tu,* enjoy the life also you! And she was gone, her leaving provoking in him a proper if gratifying distress. For he was profoundly, gustily, relieved, not only at her absence but at the prompt timetable of his pain. Nowadays he was slightly sickened whenever he remembered that voluptuous pleasure, the slow bloodletting, his ribs growing over the pulpy mess of what he was pleased to call—this word undelayed by irony—his *heart*. Oddly enough, he even understood what she meant, having been accused many times of moral rectitude.

He found it difficult now to tear open the onionskin of memory. Her face, her voice, lacked resonance, had become empty for him. The misplaced scent of pears recalled her pale instep beneath his distracted mouth. Those were the days when women wore ankle straps, walked at least two inches above the street, at variance with gravity. Still, for a journalist there had been much from which he had averted his gaze: birds smashed on frozen ground, small animals cut out against the highway, the wet-lashed eyes of beggars in the city. Pedestrians walked towards him, their faces obscured by the plumes of mist they breathed out on this cold evening. Halpern was perpetually bewildered, looked in all four directions (left, right, up, down) when he crossed the street.

It was unseasonably cold, the kind of week spoken of with pride, affection even, after the first spring thaw, but accompanied at the time by a general rhubarb of discontent and ill-humour. The winds rolled down off the arctic, bringing with them the pale blandishments of snow in a landscape already snowbound, one fall indistinguishable from the next. Like all people born in this country, Halpern was immensely, humourlessly stoic. Imagine a country blown up and down and sideways by its own vernacular, a white parallelogram, a bolt of badly sheared cloth held down by nothing but Douglas firs and the bones of old maples.

And the need to live a personal life. Halpern studied the thermometer path of the highway spread out across his knees. On a day like this there was pleasure in folding maps into precise concertinas, listening to the engine cough itself into reluctant duty. The sound of cold metal grating against its own medium recalled the interlocking cells of his body, reproducing in excess of propriety even now. But the road calmed him, the signposts that every fifty kilometres informed that he was on track, the little towns with their unpredictable names, but their predictable pride in names, as if aware of all their lost or misplaced sons and daughters moving from country to country, looking for a place that cannot be put into words.

It was such a town that Halpern grew out of, a blank-eyed, unimaginable town where the flies drowned in saucers of sugar water set on window-sills all summer long. Was memory something he had or something he lost? This was his home once, now he was back but it had gone on without him, the elms each year another ring around the collar. On the car radio a woman sang love songs in a voice indiscreet with obscure longings and partial truths. Halpern was strangely moved by her mispronunciation of the world, the quality of light falling lightly upon surfaces. An absorbed, preoccupied landscape through which he moved carefully and without emphasis, a man susceptible to Bach and God, the slight breathlessness of flowers, and the insoluble need to love.

Whenever he was asked about his childhood in that small northern town where his father was hired by what was known with local precision as The Company, he replied, a good place to live but I wouldn't want to visit. In fact he did not really mind the scuffed provincialism of small towns, the indigent grille of streets and houses tossed backwards onto the prairie, and nights shuffled between the decks of cards at Ernie's Variety Pub and Poolroom. The summer he was sixteen it rained every day. In the middle of the night he would wake to rain that had paced itself perversely to his breath. Sometimes the corrugated tin ceiling sprang a leak and his mother would run to find basins, sponges, towels. Because the rain was lonely also, it wanted to come indoors, to live plentifully. The rain that year was not without feeling.

Outside frogs turned their throats inside out, crickets whisked the air to static. The problem, although Daniel did not know this yet, was one of surfeit. Too much of everything, the rains forcing unnatural blooms from rose bushes, lilac trees, peony stems. Scent indistinguishable from scent, the thick impossibility of colour. And the girls in their summer dresses, floral prints straining across hot skin. He walked about, the year he was sixteen, dazed by the scent of mortality, the rains green, full of chlorophyll and affliction. He fell in love over and over, his progress itinerant and farcical, the nape of a neck here, the roped vertebrae on a tanned back there. Sometimes he felt what he was pleased to call his *soul* rise from its ribcage and climb up his throat to lodge in his cerebellum. At these times he could barely breathe, thinking of kisses the texture of mush-rooms, imagining the way radishes bite back.

It pained Halpern obscurely to remember that summer, the sky taut, a cowhide drum before thunder, his disordered relief when the clouds unleashed their rain. And that narrow hour of leaf-spun half-light before the night rose from the damp grass. One day a bird flew through the air vent into his bedroom and huddled on the rafters for a long time, stunned by the cloistered heat, the noise. And Daniel, plagued even then by the pity that was to haunt him, chased her about the room with a baseball cap, her wings snapping against the air. He carried her out in one hand, his fingers cupped about her wings, a thin grey head poking through the hollow of thumb and forefinger. The nomadic pulse that beat into his cupped hand that day woke him from tapering dreams even after he had long forgotten the incident.

His father was to remain in that town for the rest of a life cut graphically short by something terminal and uncompromising and which, they were assured by The Company, had no connection at all to the smoke-stacked compound in which he spent his working days. His mother followed shortly after, more from habit than necessity, which provided at least a pattern by means of which Daniel could mourn their loss. Their passing from the world with such reticent good-humour, such well-mannered pain, did not, however, provide for him the limit he desired. Do not appear if you do not want to disappear. That was what their example came down to in the end, and Daniel couldn't help feeling a sense of bathos at their indeterminate lives cropped to aphorism. In the crescent cut-out of night leaves that summer, fruit bats flickered, the shadow of an owl moved silently over uneven grass, but when Daniel looked up, there was nothing to see. This was the way time passed, like an owl that could never be caught except in the progress of its flight, only at certain times, and always from the corner of the eye.

As Halpern drove, his hands beating against the steering wheel in time to the car radio, his body remembered other highways, different cars, *it's that old déjà-vu all over again,* he sang in uncharacteristic exuberance, *all over and over and over again*. Annex was no different to the other towns he passed, preceded by a graveyard for dead cars and a sign that said "slow to 40 km." Along the shoulder of the road, rusty metal carcasses aligned themselves with the embankment, diminished by time and neglect. At a certain point in the journey the railway tracks doubled back on themselves and were suddenly visible from the road, a set of paired footnotes trailing over the print-out of snow and telephone wires.

Like other towns, Annex was bisected by the highway, on either side low-lying buildings crouched against the strident persuasion of the horizontal plane: a hospital, a single storied care home, a windowless school-house, a main street composed of two banks, three food stores, a building that housed both the Annex Free Press and Ruhudsky's Hardware, a thrift store, a laundromat and a dingy café into which customers were ushered by a large, well-dressed chicken. None of the town's four churches and one Interfaith Hall were in evidence as Halpern pulled up to the parking lot of the only motor hotel. The Number Eight was cluttered with television aerials and neon-blinking Coke dispensers, and an old man in a snow suit lounging on his balcony. Halpern had the feeling that the man with his sweat-stained baseball cap and ears reddened by cold or anger, was as much a fixture at the Number Eight as the all-year Christmas lights and the secondhand washing machine perched desultorily on a snow bank. He had the strongest sense that life had slowed down imperceptibly, that the black and white panorama before him had been mysteriously enlarged so that the grain of the paper was apparent underneath. The old man squinted fiercely at his number plate but otherwise made no gesture of greeting.

The woman behind the desk was thin and quick-bodied. "Oh, you're that journalist come up to see the blood girl." In one oddly hungry movement she took a key from the board behind her and pushed the guest register towards him. "Sign there, and there, no liquor in the rooms and you can park— yes, behind is fine."

Inside the motel the air was lungy, the carpet threadbare with the passage of transient feet. Halpern, an incurable reader, noticed at once the sign tacked to the right of the half-open elevator doors: This Machine will not Work on the Day of Ascension! At the other end of the lobby a row of public telephones kept their own counsel. At one of them, a man with the glitter of cheap gold about fingers and wrist shouted corpulent directives into the mouthpiece. The salesman was plush, almost upholstered, and he mouthed an expletive into the receiver before hanging up.

The woman behind the counter at the Number Eight shrugged, her conversation truncated by Halpern's arrival. Her eyes were curiously avid, lit by some troubling question, but she made no further gesture. Halpern nodded, signed, shoul- dered his overnight bag. He was halfway to the door when her next remark reached him, addressed to someone beyond the half-opened door in the room behind, but audible. "That child's too much trouble for any town to bear."

As he felt so often in a new place, before the story had properly begun, Halpern was awed by his own presumption, by his lack of intentionality. At these times he fell back upon his orderly habits: he flossed his teeth or put together a deftly cut salad, forced himself through a Baroque fugue complete with sheet music. Today in this motel room cobbled from disillusioned colours, with the sound of air opening and closing erratically behind semi-trailers on the highway, he took out the research notes he acquired from the newspaper archives and compiled a list.

<u>The Markings of the Stigmata</u>

1) Replicas of the wounds of Christ's death
   – marks in the hands as if nails have been hammered through
   – ditto in the feet. These can
   i) bleed
   ii) seep clear fluid
   iii) take the form of bruise-like impressions of the heads of
        nails, round and black, standing clear from the flesh

2) Somatic markings that replicate Christ's suffering
   – wounding of the right side, usually taking the form of a
     bleeding crescent
   – marks on forehead corresponding to those made by a crown
     of thorns or else forming a red cross
   – stripes across the back as if from scourging
   – deformation of right shoulder as if a heavy object has been
     carried for some distance

3) Mysterious features accompanying these signs
   – a fragrance of roses or incense at the time of bleeding
   – the bodies of stigmatics remaining supple and
     undecomposed after death

4) Asomatic occurrences
   – cases of pious individuals reporting pain in hands and feet
     but producing no marks.

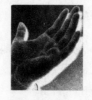

Halpern

After examining the list for some moments Halpern drew the page towards him and wrote rapidly:

> There must be cases of stigmata which have occurred and been kept secret. Although it seems difficult to imagine how a conspicuous set of marks can be kept secret, especially if they survive on the body and are present at death.

As well as his research notes and a manually operated camera, Halpern had brought a sheaf of case-histories gathered from diverse sources: newspaper archives, encyclopedias, and religious journals. He drew one of these last towards him, *The Churchman's Companion*, a glossy publication on expensive paper, and began to read an article entitled "Christ's Wounds in the Middle Ages."

> In the first half of the thirteenth century, a Praemonstratensian monk was killed beneath the collapsed wall of a ruin. Brother Dodo had led a solitary life and when his body was

removed from the rubble, open wounds corresponding to the five wounds of the crucifixion were discovered. The monks who were responsible for his laying out were astonished, especially since it had not been known during his lifetime that he was the bearer of such beatitude. At first they hailed him as the precursor to St. Francis of Assisi, whose body was similarly inscribed with the five marks of passion. Later scholars, however, have been hesitant to interpret the wounds in this manner since it is possible that they were self-inflicted as part of the Monk's devotion to the Passion. In 1268, St. Christina of Stommeln received similar wounds in hands, feet, side, as well as upon her forehead. Being of a pious and retiring nature, she attempted to keep them secret but was not successful. Stories spread—

There was a scrabbling at the door, Halpern fell out of this glazed Medieval world full of bloody souls, and back into a makeshift room on the edge of the highway. A muffled voice, a message pushed awkwardly beneath the door. The doctor who attended Donna Desjardins would see him at midday. ∎

Transcript of Interview between Dr. Virginie Waters and Daniel Halpern: Annex Hospital, May 4th: 12:30 p.m.

VW. I should say at the outset that I'm not quite sure what your interest is in this matter. Yes, I know, a journalist, but why now, when the phenomena has apparently ceased and everything's back to normal? It must be, what—two, three weeks since Easter? Even the newspaper articles have died down. Aah well—what would you like?

DH. *A diagnosis, perhaps?*

VW. The patient presented to me with blood freely flowing from an off-centre position on the palm of her left hand, followed in a matter of hours by the same on the right hand. There were no lesions apparent then or at any time after. Although the specific symbolism of the purpura is in question I think it would not be an exaggeration to say the "wounds" were produced by an act of empathy.

DH. *For whom?*

VW. Well that's a matter of opinion.

DH. *In your opinion then?*

VW. Look, Mr. Halpern, there's a standard diagnosis in such cases. I'm sure you've read it many times in the newspapers over the last fortnight. Lesions may be described as a necrosis of the epidermis of neurotic origin, a symmetrical arrangement probably attributable to suggestion.

DH. *But that's the profile of an adult stigmatic, isn't it? See, I have my own notes: "spontaneous lesions usually preceded by psychological trauma." Yet we're speaking of an eleven-year-old girl. A child who seemed to be remarkably healthy and well-adjusted until the moment when she began bleeding.*

VW. Make a long arm Mr. Halpern, and pass me that folder, yes over there. Do you see what this is [she holds up a child's drawing], this is what Donna was occupying herself with at the time of the— the presentation. And she is a dear child, yes, you will see. Such frank eyes and always balancing on one foot or the other. Pictures of a Madonna and Child. Well, there's plenty of evidence for the inexplicable. Perhaps it's Father Ricci you should be speaking to. I don't have the language to explain mysticism.

DH. *Tell me, Dr. Waters, what are the odds of an eleven-year-old child beating herself up for God?*

VW. You're suggesting—what? Previous traumas or the fantasies of a masochist? Which one? I tell you Mr. Halpern, that child is a recycled angel. I mean that in the most secular sense of the word.

DH. *Multiple personality then?*

VW. Where do you people learn these words?

DH. *Well there was an article in the* Archives of Internal Medicine *making a tentative connection between these phenomena and . . . that while the . . . subject in one personality undergoes a vision later recalled by the self, another self exists which physically marks the body and which the normal self doesn't recall having made.*

VW. Yes, or she could just have been a unicorn. That's what I call these patients. They come into our lives without warning and leave just as suddenly. I know this sounds fanciful, Mr. Halpern, but to me she is a unicorn and what's more, a perfectly healthy unicorn. There won't be another episode of the bleeding. Of course, that's only my hunch, not a medical diagnosis. And now a question from me. What is the importance of authenticity?

DH. *Well the question of physical intervention is key. If it can be proven, then it's assumed the experience is fraudulent, or at least of little consequence.*

VW. What you're looking for is a space in which to enter? There are many ways of learning. We can learn from pleasure, from pain. You, Mr. Halpern, you are quite well? Physically, I mean. If you have ever suffered from illness, an outbreak of careless writing on the body, you will realize what I mean. Do you know that in medieval times these people—stigmatics—were called wounded healers. To heal others it was thought the subject needed to be broken open.

DH. *Dr. Waters, has anything like this happened here before?*

VW. No, not in my time. But I've been here only for the last two years.

DH. *But you have access to archival records don't you? And you seem to be interested in the subject.*

VW. You're right. I looked, even found something. Since you ask I'll tell you. In 1933 a Ukrainian woman, Alisha Hukic, was admitted to the hospital with symptoms that indicate she was suffering from advanced multiple sclerosis. She was in her late forties and could speak no English. Her husband, a farmer, was marginally more fluent and so acted as translator. She remained in permanent care for six months, as we had no Care Home in those days. One morning after a particularly severe night of pain, the nurses came to change her bedding only to find that her hands were bleeding. Her wounds opened and closed, bled and re-opened, until her death one year later. The marks on her palms were the size of dimes and there were the beginnings of similar markings on her feet. In addition, she had a permanent form of bruising around her wrist that appeared to be a rope burn.

DH. *How was she diagnosed?*

VW. The medical notes are sparse and incredulous but there is an aside to the effect that when she was initially examined, there was no evidence of obsessive scratching or other acts of self-mutilation. This would seem to indicate that the examining physician, Dr. Isaacs, did not suspect her of any psychological disorder. Anyway, as an MS patient she would not have had strength to make the marks.

DH. *They simply appeared?*

VW. They appeared spontaneously after a night of pain while she was in hospital and under constant observation. When she died twelve months later, the marks remained on her body as a transparency of the tissues.

DH. *And Dr. Isaacs?*

VW. Is dead. His daughter is alive, though. I think she lives in the Personal Care Home. Listen, the two cases are unconnected. Yet I took the trouble to look. Yes, I can see what your face is saying, Mr. Halpern. How does the poet put it, *I give you the end of a golden thread to lead you into the day.* Blake. Something like that.

———— End of Transcript ————

Halpern

A f t e r stopping at the Number Eight to collect his camera, after a lunch of indifferently sliced turkey sandwiches, Halpern set off to traverse the town. It was bone-cold but the wind had lifted a little. The main street, inexplicably called Walnut Avenue, began with the school yard, filled with children in groups of three and five. Halpern scanned the flushed faces framed by toques and scarves in convivial colours. He was looking for the equivalent of the grainy black and white newspaper photograph, the child with shocked, widely spaced eyes and a blur of dark hair. But the bundled children did not allow for individuality, and he had already turned away when, out of the clatter and throb of playground noises, he heard a thin voice calling an indistinguishable name. At the far end of the school yard a girl in a dark blue jacket turned on the pivot of her heel to respond to her playmate. At the same moment, a teacher hurried out of the entrance, agitated no doubt by the unknown man gazing at the children, his wind-chaffed knuckles thrust between the chicken wire fencing.

At the corner of Walnut and Elm, Halpern saw the spire of Our Lady of Perpetual Mercy and All Saints that the woman at the Number Eight had told him would be kitty-corner to the curling rink and across from Johanson's Funeral Home. The church was a gabled structure with a mock-epic false front grafted onto the squat unlikeliness of a prairie dancehall. Against the gathering sky the dark crucifix at the top of the spire cast a laconic shadow. Halpern unhitched his camera and framed the image before pushing open the door and hurrying into comparative warmth and light. It was a church like any other, reticent and emphatic. The pews were empty save for an old woman who knelt at the back, hiding her face between cupped palms. On the walls hung a series of exceedingly weary saints looking into the vanishing point of empty skies. The door to the chancellery was locked and a handwritten notice advised that Father Massimo Ricci was out of town for the afternoon but would be back to take evening service at six o'clock. Halpern, who had never been into a church for any reason save architectural, whose relationship with God was, he believed, congenially indifferent, nevertheless wandered skittishly towards the altar. A last fall of light gathered against the background of white linen and burnt-out candles, seeming to force a gesture of reluctant awe from the viewer. Using his flash bulb, he took a shorthand photograph, but already the back of his neck was prickly with agnostic self-consciousness and he hurried towards the door and the more ascetic excesses of snow and wind. The kneeling woman did not raise her eyes as the door swung back upon its well-oiled joints.

Halpern had almost forgotten the sediment of half past four on a winter's day when the streets have thinned of school children and the pick-up trucks along Railway Avenue have begun to line up outside Bill's Yard and Pool Room. How the light thickened for a few seconds, postponing that abstract moment when darkness fell. He was thinking of the picture of the Madonna and Child that Dr. Waters showed him, and an earlier image that remained, of Michelangelo's Pietà. What impressed him when he first saw her, the marble Madonna in St. Peter's Cathedral, was her outflung left hand, empty. As if with this gesture she were saying, see what I have lost, see how I unclench my hands even in the presence of grief.

Back in his motel room Halpern was unsuccessful at reaching the Desjardins household. Since they had not returned any of the calls he placed from the city, he anticipated a reluctance to submit themselves to further interviews, especially since the wounds had healed, the school term started again, and even Father Ricci had business elsewhere. Instead, he placed a call to the Personal Care Home and was somewhat luckier. "Sure we can always do with company, come over at about five-thirty, that's when they've eaten," said a breathless voice in answer to his query about Mina Isaacs, daughter of the late doctor.

The interior of the Care Home was institutional green but fresh flowers clustered at the reception desk and children's drawings decorated the walls. After an effusive greeting from the nurse on duty, who seemed to feel that he must be a relative from the city, Halpern found Mina Isaacs in the common room.

A minutely creased old woman with a surprisingly fresh, crumpled rosebud of a mouth in the desert of her face she was about eighty years old, small and immeasurably shrunken, held together by nothing so much as the heavy folds of her corded dressing-gown.

"Sit down," she gestured at Halpern. "Don't be afraid to come in, I won't fall apart. Still," she added, "sometimes I think I should have kept the body I started with."

The nurse hurriedly handed Halpern a mug of coffee in her distracted progress through the room, and Mina Isaacs took it from him, holding it between arthritic hands to warm them. Her voice rustled like tissue paper, the story she told emerging breathlessly from its wrappings. ▌

Transcript of Interview between Mina Isaacs and Daniel Halpern: Annex Personal Care Home, May 4th: 5:30 p.m.

MI. What can I tell you about those days? On Sunday mornings I lie in bed long after I should. The moment before I am properly awake is the time I choose to push myself against the skin of memory that keeps me in this world. I want to lay my head on someone's shoulder, take a deep breath, say *enough*.

Well, enough. I was born here, in the new world, but my mother was a girl with Alisha Hukic when they left their homeland after the famine and the uprisings. On the long march out they ate leaves with salt on them, unripe apples, rotting onions dug up at night from the fields. Alisha was very weak, very sick. She said over and over again, I want to go home. Over and over. My mother took her by the arm, shook her. She said, There is no home, there is no Laskia.

Well then, they came here together, to this country. The government was offering money and share-holdings for people willing to go west and populate the prairies, so they married men from the old country and came to live here. When you have lost your first home there is no other. Still, they built houses and had children. I myself was the first daughter born from this soil. My father, who studied to be a doctor, would say, Land round here grows nothing but rocks! But my mother, she and I, we knew different.

And then Alisha got ill, she had to go and live in the hospital. All these years and still not a word of English. The nurses couldn't understand her. And she could not understand. My mother would go often to sit with her. At first they would speak of the old days, of the storks that roosted in the chimneys, and the taste of caraway bread that puckers the mouth. But then the pain would get bad, very bad, and my mother would go running for the nurse.

The day of the bleeding now, yes I remember. It was the week before Easter, my mother was sitting with Alisha when the nurses came to change the bedding. They turned her over and her hands were full of blood. One nurse put her finger right in the wounds. What is this? she asked my mother. My mother told her, but the nurse looked at her blankly because she had not heard the word before.

My father was angry, *mad*, that is the right word? A childhood in the Ukraine with nothing but skin and bones, and then this country, the hard years when he was the only doctor for miles around and still the people couldn't pay for his services and he grew thin with holding the world together in his hands. In all of this he was good-humoured, enjoyed a joke, a glass of apricot brandy with the men on a Saturday night. After Alisha Hukic began to bleed from the palms of her hands something in him darkened, grew bitter. His medicine couldn't explain so he pretended he couldn't understand. And yet, not once, never once if he was honest with himself, could he doubt what he saw. Once I heard him say to my mother, I was a girl but I still remember: You don't have to believe in something to be frightened of it—it's two different parts of the brain.

My mother of course remained devoted to Alisha, they were friends from the old country. There was no pattern, no period to the bleeding, the wounds would be closed for weeks at a time and then one day, blood on the sheets. Sometimes when they were sitting together my mother would be aware of a scent like roses, or was it spice? Very soon she came to associate this smell with the times that

Alisha Hukic began to bleed. As for Alisha, she was in great pain and often she would not speak for days. But she told my mother that when she bled heavily it was a sign someone close would die. One night a young girl in the ward next door came to her. I won't be here tomorrow, I won't be here tomorrow, I won't be here tomorrow, she said. The next morning she was dead and Alisha's hands were full of blood. My father said such things were old wives' tales. The young girl was paralyzed and could not have come to Alisha's bedside. The bleeding itself was natural, necessary even, if only such things could be understood. The body had its own laws, its own fluctuations. My father grew more angry every day.

I don't remember when she died. Her life was so extraordinary, you see, it blotted out her death. Quite soon afterwards, I think. I remember her funeral because that was when I first saw Regina Arnott. She was Alisha's niece come to live on the Hukic farm after her mother died. A slip of a girl. Like a leaf, something you'd find slipped between the storm windows. She's a great big woman now, so they tell me, but then she was a tiny thing and she stood on one leg in front of the grave with a dirty face. Aah well.

Oh, one other thing. Alisha Hukic cured my mother's arthritis. My mother had it bad, like I do now. Could hardly do up her buttons. One night Alisha reached down and took hold of my mother's stiff wrists in her own hands. My mother said they sat like that for hours, at first she felt nothing and then a kind of warmth reaching up from her fingertips. Alisha just lay there with her eyes shut, holding onto my mother's wrists, and hours went by and in the morning my mother woke up for the first time in years without pain. The swelling in the joints had gone down and her fingers were more flexible than they'd ever been. She began to work up a pair of slippers for my father in needlepoint but he never wore them because by then he was so angry he hardly came home. Luckily, Alisha Hukic died shortly after-wards and my parents were able to get on with their lives. My mother began to sew a memory quilt. My father stayed home in the evenings, reading the newspaper with his feet up on an ottoman.

Do you know, it's years since I remembered those funny old slippers embroidered with arum lilies and violets. Something happens when you get to my age, you've no memory for details, for satin stitch and velvet, or how tall grass feels against your cheek on an itchy day in midsummer. All my dreams are in black and white these days, like the old movies we used to watch down at the church hall. Aah well, she cured us all in the end, Alisha. She cured me of religion, and mum of her arthritis, and dad of disbelief. Everyone but herself. She cured everyone but herself.

———— End of Transcript ————

H a l p e r n

I n h i s most recent exile, Halpern sat at a desk in his motel room. Tired and listless, he took out a notebook and began to jot down his impressions of Virginie Waters and Mina Isaacs. Outside his window the highway was illuminated by the anesthetic light of stars which did not penetrate his room, insulated as it was by the static hum of the ice-machine down the hall. A single neon tube scrawled the name of the motel over and over, cursive and intermittent into the sky. ∎

Worknotes

Virginie Waters

- One of those antiseptic citrus-flavoured women caught somewhere between skepticism and empiricism. She does not for a moment believe what she saw.

- Wears a white medical smock and latex gloves throughout the interview as if she believes speech is contagious.

- Obviously researched spontaneous lesions after treating Donna Desjardins. Highly protective of Donna (of all her patients perhaps?) so protective in fact, that she is willing to indulge in fanciful and uncharacteristic speculations of the unicorn variety.

- Her painstaking avoidance of words like God, Christ, Jesus, etc.

Mina Isaacs

- She has learned to unclench her fists, she is a woman who waves goodbye with her hands open. Told me she lost her husband and only son in a farming accident ten years ago. A daughter who lives in Ontario, they write to each other. After all, what can a body do? she asked me, what is there to do? You can't stop others from leaving. The trick is to begin missing them while they are still there.

- The impression one has of a story blown out, supple as a balloon, from that oddly fresh mouth.

Halpern

Between the sporadic hiss of trucks on the highway, the clink of glass and occasional laughter rising below his room. Suddenly lonely, Halpern washed his face, decided to have a late night drink. A minor shuffle at his entrance but conversation resumed on the next beat, a subtle atonality of voices punctuated by the sharp tick of a pool cue and the drone of VLT machines along the far wall. As he walked past, two older men in overalls with baseball caps pulled low over their foreheads returned to the subject at hand.

"So doc says he's got to have it out, something internal."

"What? What's he got coming out?"

"Not sure. Pity, but."

"Pity."

The barkeeper slid him a beer and gave him a "new here?" look but made no comment. Halpern's pupils widened to adjust to the underwater light as the woman who had earlier checked him in walked forward.

"Get you anything? Want I should fix a sandwich?" She

had expanded in the smoky, humid air of the bar as if night was her medium.

"No thanks." But she sat down beside him anyhow.

"Any luck with the blood girl?"

"No, I can't get hold of her mother."

"Well you can't blame them really. All through Easter you guys were three deep in this town, good for business, but. Nope, only way you're going to see that family now, I reckon, is through Father Ricky."

"He new?"

"He's the Catholic priest, got some Eyetalian name no-one can pronounce but a nice guy, a kidder. Always trying to teach me Eyetalian, says if I learn I'll make better cappuccino. Anyways, ever since that blood business he and the family been real close. Who'd you go and see today?"

Clearly there was to be a *quid* to this *pro quo*, Halpern did not demur for long.

"Dr. Waters."

"Doctor Ginny we say round here on account of her father was the real Doc Waters."

"Her father works in this town?"

"Used to. Died five years ago. Fact, Doctor Ginny was born right here. Didn't stay long, though. Her mum took her out to Québec when she was only three, they left the old Doc, went to join her family out East. Then two years ago she came back to work in the Annex Clinic, no-one knows why, a bright girl like that. Anyways, you won't get anything out of her, she doesn't hold with such things. Went to see her last year on account of getting married. Thought I'd get myself fixed up properly instead of those rubber things feel like a wet sock going in. I'm getting married tomorrow afternoon, I told her, can you write me a prescription for the pill. Laughed so hard she almost fell off her chair. Here, Delma, she said, but you got to take 'em for a month before you're safe. I saw the joke although Jim thought she was being disrespectful. Still, you got to be careful with things like that, some people'd say she was showing ignorance. Never been anywhere, my Jim, that's the problem. Stays put like his dad he's the chip off. Look, we're closing in half an hour, want a glassful of anything else?"

She began to wipe down the counter in front of him with quick awkward circles of her wrist. The fake leather counter top puckered into smears of moisture in the wake of her damp cloth. Halpern bought a beer for himself, another for her.

"Do you know the Desjardins at all?"

"Know of them. Know of everyone here. There's only six hundred of us after all. But they're Catholics and stick to their own. The mother works at the hospital. Mum knew her from there, they were both cleaners. She still is, mum's retired though. Don't know anything against them except for the son. He's an idiot boy but not violent, one of them Mongoloids. Strange to look at, that bulging forehead, web-fingers, the lot. Not his fault, but. Used to see Donna walking to the post-office with him in the afternoons. Terribly careful of him, used to hold his hand all the way there and back, talking in a quiet kind of voice like you use with frightened horses. He adored her, my Dawnie, he'd call her. But we don't see much of either of them after that business. I suppose they're ashamed of themselves."

She wound a strand of hair round her index finger as she spoke. Halpern watched as the curl sprang back into place. Her nail beds were beautifully cultivated, each oval buffed to a deep pink gloss.

"You think the bleeding was a hoax?"

"No, but mischief all the same. The whole town in an uproar and television crews coming down and messing up the rooms and flirting with the staff. They say she lost so much blood she almost died. Her mum had to change the sheets twice a day, they were soaked through. Anyways, I don't think there was anything magical about it. Not *religious* magical at any rate. Like mum says, young girls of that age they have powers. They're just starting to grow up and, well, maybe it's like in the movies. Poltergeists is what they call them."

This last was pronounced with distracted authority and Halpern saw that her eyes were fixed on an older woman at the far end of the bar. She had been sitting alone drinking steadily, a brimming, barefoot kind of woman, although in fact she wore men's socks inside stout work boots, and her hair was thatched, hung about her face like eaves. Her nocturnal eyes looked stunned even in the muted light of the bar. Halpern watched her turn to the man beside her.

"Want to see a match burn twice?"

"Sure."

She struck a kitchen match on the wood of her stool, blew it out, then quickly and with impersonal spite, jabbed him in the wrist with the burning head. The man exclaimed and jerked his hand away.

"Mean drunk that one," Delma muttered beside Halpern, "though you wouldn't know she was drunk to talk to."

"Who is she?"

"Name's Regina Arnott, lives over by the trailer park. Crazy woman but harmless mostly."

Nothing Halpern had seen so far convinced him of the sagacity of this statement but one of the VLT machines began to spit coins and Delma hurried over to investigate.

"Want to see a match burn twice?" She regarded him with humorous disdain, a con already in sight of her mark.

"No but I'll buy you a drink."

"Surely."

In one unbroken and surprisingly lovely arc she poured the liquid from the glass down her throat, eggshell and tender in the light. "Hell, if you throw in a pickled egg I'll even tell you a story."

Halpern gestured to the bartender who frothed her a beer, then fished wearily in a one gallon jar full of peeled eggs, peppercorns and brine. It was that part of the evening when the bar had thinned to serious drinkers, gamblers, and insomniacs, but the air was still heavy with smoke, a disembodied and impersonal nostalgia.

"This is a story about flowers," she began. ∎

Story told to Daniel Halpern by Regina Arnott

In this town the women are bitter and tannic as slow-steeped tea
but the men are flat beer, spilt beer. The men wear their eyes sideways and scratch with blind fingers at their groins. Looking for their
balls, someone once said, and it is a joke in the town although no-
one has ever told it, that the only male with balls worth speaking of
spent his last days tied by the collar to the door frame of Ed's Dry
Good's Store. But Ed's Doberman has been dead for some two years
now and no-one tells that joke no more no more, not since Ed's wife
fell down the cellar stairs and broke two ribs and blackened both
eyes and left town for the women's shelter in the city and was never
heard from again.

Down at the general hospital the doctor works behind closed
doors, palpating and probing, the old doc that is, looking for suspi-
cious lumps and lesions and ligaments, all the slipped stitches of the
bodies unraveled before him on the examination table. Ho-hum,
the doctor puts one eye to his silver speculum, smile for the camera,
he chants gaily. His secretary sits in the reception area upright as a
teapot. All day she fills out forms listening to the talk of the waiting
room, the farmers who gather on wet days in a warm place till the
motel cocktail lounge opens for the afternoon.

"How's the crop comin?"

"It's comin."

"How's your back goin?"

"It's goin."

"How's the wife doin?"

"She's doin."

Nothing comin, nothing goin, nothing doin.

Years ago the train, bright as a silver needle, would dart through the town twice a week, weaving an embroidery of smoke in the sky as it passed. Now only the railway tracks remain, like a double row of stitches. A man walks brusquely into the waiting room, his trousers rasping against his thighs with each irritated step. I want to speak to the man in charge, he tells the doctor's secretary.

He is a stranger in the town, a passer-through, a fly-by-nighter, a here-today-gone-tomorrower, and the woman who limps after him is also a stranger, although there are one hundred and twenty-two others just like her in this town. Somewhere south of plump with a coarse-woven soft-textured body that she wears like a turn-of-the-season pullover. All the pleasure in her world to be found in those four spoonfuls of sugar that she takes in her afternoon tea. And her morning tea too, if the truth be known, how she stirs and stirs the sweetness in, nothing else nothing since gonna taste so sweet baby sweet sweetsweet.

Take a seat, says the doctor's secretary, the doctor will see you presently. Later, the strangers are seen at Turkle's pharmacy where again the man strides forward, demanding to see the man in charge. And has a prescription filled out for penicillin, stopping to flip a gross of Trojans at the cashier. They're seen again at the bank, the Co-op store, the gas station. He withdraws two hundred dollars from a savings account in Alberta, buys three sticks of barbecued jerky, and fills his pick-up with regular unleaded, best of Steve's Texaco. All this the town knows by nightfall. The woman follows him and this the town also knows. She is a silent letter, the u in quiet.

The last place they're seen is the cocktail lounge at the Number

Eight, last pumpstop for three hundred and fifty miles on the dry
run to Thompson, at two in the morning, where it is told, a strange
incident occurred. It was that time of the evening when the air is
grained with smoke and whiskey, and the game has just ended on
the outsize TV screen in the corner. Nothing to watch but the horses
with their scornful names: *Lofty Stallion, Golden Crescent,
Bumptious Boy.* Time for a hand-me-down or a pick-me-up, time for
a shot or a slug or a shooter, time before time's up, goodnight ladies
and god bless you merry gentlemen. The barmaids at the Sharptail
Shooter Pub and Poolroom push pencils through hair matted with
smoke and sweat and hurriedly get their last orders in while Barnard
the barkeep starts in on his boasting, telling about the housewives
whose boilers he comes to stoke between October and March each
year, his dad taught him that. And how to choose a dog and lose
a wife. How to stay put, upright at least, never mind being second
hand, third rate.

And maybe it's this that inflames the stranger so, or Barnard
taking nonevermind of his repeated order for another rye, or the
barmaid everyone calls Barnard's girl forgetting his soda. Or maybe
it's the woman who has limped behind him all day, now slouching
sidesaddle on a barstool, her lower lip puckered against the cold
glass. Maybe it's this makes him shout suddenly into the flickering
silence contracting like a shrinking dot on the TV screen, that makes
him shout suddenly into the silence that shrinks him like a dot, that
makes him shout:

I want to speak to the man in charge!

In the silence that follows a woman begins to sing.

I want to speak to the man in cha-arge
I want to speak to the man in cha-arge
I want to speak to the man in cha-arge
    OR
The wo-man who knows who he is!

In the silence that follows a woman begins to laugh.

It's the same woman, it's the stranger's woman sitting sidesaddle on her barstool, knees puffed as hot pies as she throws back her head and laughs, throws back her head and her chins and her shoulders and laughs like shook down. In the dim half-light she sings:

    OR
The wo-man who knows who he is!

That laugh, that laugh, I want to tell you about that laugh, how it flew through the town infecting the women as they slept, how it took root and blossomed in the rich dark loam of their mouths, how they laughed in their dreams, how they laughed in their sleep, how they laughed all the heaving night away. Somewhere in the distance a train whistle sounded and a silver train darted quick as a needle through the suede of the night and the women awoke with laughter seeding their throats.

Wish I could tell how that laughter sang in the whole town's bones all that day and the next, how the women grew flowers in their hair, how they told jokes in the street and doubled their knees and shucked their shoulders and covered their open mouths with wet fingers, how they pointed at the men, this one and that one, and yelled across balconies or down alleys or from windows *lookin' for their balls eh, lookin' for their balls.* How the women grew mouse-traps and how they laughed at the men caught fast by the little bit of cheese between their laughing thighs. How the doctor's secretary put a notice above her desk reading *would you like to speak to the man in charge, or the woman who knows who he is?* How the barkeep's girl changed her name to Camellia and took herself a boy. How they laughed, the women, how they laughed and sang.

But the stranger quieted his woman with an impatient backhand. *Swat swat,* and that was all. That is all.

Oh yes, the flowers.

Many flowers were planted that night in the eyes of the women by the men with clenchfists. And they bloomed through the day these flowers.

Halpern

H i s   b o d y heavy, full of sediment, Halpern woke the
moment a skein of geese wedged north, past his window.
Huddled in his jacket, he hurried across the highway to Jeane's
Bake Shop and ordered coffee and toast, a couple of eggs. It
was early in the morning but the café was already full of men
in overalls and lumber jackets, and the air was humid with the
steam from their coffee. A couple of truckers were teasing the
waitress, who leaned on one leg with her hip thrust forward to
take their order.

"Kind of eggs you got, sweetheart?"

No-one took any notice of him. Halpern warmed his
hands around the thick mug he was handed, and folded gratefully into isolation, the precision of lists. ▋

Halpern's List of Questions, Oddities and Strange Occurrences

1) What the hell is a blood miracle?

2) Why did Virginie Waters come back to take over her father's practice? Pilgrimage or atonement?

3) What has Alisha Hukic to do with anything? Can a case be made for locality? A small town in which two stigmatics— over a period of sixty years—have lived, is surely significant.

    But Alisha Hukic was an immigrant, a woman without language, middle-aged and suffering from a terminal condition. Donna Desjardins is eleven years old, physically healthy, by all reports emotionally stable. Their only point of contact is that both suffered in the weeks before Easter from inexplicable wounds.

4) Who is Regina Arnott? As Alisha's niece does she have special knowledge? What did she mean by telling me that story? Is she supposed to be the woman who followed the stranger into town?

5) Need to find out more about stigmata. Contact that Helena person at the gallery in Winnipeg.

Halpern

F a t h e r Ricci lived on the thick white slice of street behind
his church. The door to the green clapboard house, set well
back from the road was opened by an older woman with
gnarled hair and thick skin ploughed by irrigation lines and a
tentative smile. "Come in, *avanti,* I will show you to his study.
Massimo," she called, "your visitor."

She leaned back against the door frame as Halpern passed
through, catching a lift of stewing tomatoes and something like
fennel from her skirts. The Father, lounging in his capacious
chair, gestured toward Halpern with a gilded fountain pen.
"Come in, come in, I was just writing a letter to my Archbishop.
Madre said you called this morning."

A large, blocky man with odd pockets of flesh and fold,
Father Ricci had fashioned his room from all that was luxuri-
ous in his faith: deep pile carpets, embroidered pillows, the air
carnal with incense and a deceptively pure tenor piping from
concealed speakers. He greeted Halpern with wide arms and an
hospitable smile, settled him into an armchair with many half-

finished, annotated gestures of goodwill. He had a hearty, well-aged voice, suggestive of nothing so much as good beef and when he turned slightly to pull down a blind, Halpern noticed the thickening roll at the back of his neck.

"In Italy, where *Madre* grew up and where I was born, there's a verb used strictly for the purpose of one who stands on a balcony and watches passersby. In this country we have no balconies, we take tea, and tell each other stories."

Indeed, half an hour into the interview Signora Ricci pushed her way into the room wheeling a tray piled with china teacups, fragrant tea in a coddled pot, freshly baked scones, and an improbable mound of butter. ▌

Transcript of Interview between Father Massimo Ricci and Daniel Halpern: Ricci Home, May 5th: 10 a.m.

DH. *Father Ricci, what occurred in this town is a story that requires deep faith to be believed.*

MR. Deep faith, yes, but there is no mistaking the blood, there is no mistaking the body of the stigmatic.

DH. *And the body of this stigmatic?*

MR. For the stigmatic, love explains all, there is an extraordinary desire to be like Him, to endure in the body, in the soul, what He endured. Then there is the opposite of faith, the false stigmata, a counterfeit inspired by the devil. Consider for example the Indian rope trick: a boy nimbly climbs a length of rope suspended in the air. But if you were to take a photograph, if you were to have the film developed, you would see no evidence on the negative of any rope suspended in the air.

DH. *You're saying the stigmata is a trick, something performed under hypnosis?*

MR. No, no. Listen, a person undergoing a deep religious experience can have profound effects on the physical world. A young girl sits in her classroom, her left palm begins to itch. A blister appears, size of a ten-cent piece with a halo-shaped mark around it. Within hours the tender skin seeps blood. Such extravagant religious devotion is not everyone's cup of tea, but unless you live near a railway line you will not see trains pass your window. Faith is a talent, like everything else. You have to relax, give yourself over to it. What is it the Inuit say when they are sculpting from rock? *Release the bird from the stone.* After all, it is not only we who must believe in God, but God who exists by believing in us.

DH. *I'm not sure I understand—*

MR. I will tell you of my hero, Padre Pio. The good Father lived near Foggia in Italy. He carried the marks for fifty years. At the height of their activity, it is said they seeped a cupful of blood a day. The first time the stigmata occurred it happened quite suddenly, like an unexpected blow, during thanksgiving after Mass. Padre Pio fell to his knees, his eyes closed and his whole body trembling as if it had been broken. During the medical examination that followed, a clinical thermometer proved unable to register the high temperature of the Padre's body. Indeed, the instrument was eventually broken open by the abnormal expansion of mercury in the tube. If you go, as I went, to Foggia, you may see it, a little twist of metal and glass turned relic to commemorate the body that rejected it. Now if I were to play the devil's advocate, a case could be made for auto-suggestion, for self-mutilation. Say the good Father was a charlatan, a devil, say he fooled not only others but himself. And yet, do you know, for as many years as his wounds remained open they never became septic. Remarkable indeed, don't you think? That wounds which have been self-inflicted should show no signs of inflammation, infection or even of healing, for over half a century.

DH. *What happened to him?*

MR. He died. That's when the real story begins. It is only after death that a saintly man or woman is investigated by the Catholic Church. Stigmatization is no evidence, you see, in the Vatican's eyes, of those qualities which may result in canonization. Padre Pio is currently under investigation, but who knows what will happen, as, ironically, the Church views claims of the miraculous with extreme caution.

DH. *Where does Donna Desjardins fit in?*

MR. For every stigmatic who dies, so legend goes, another is born. There are always twelve stigmatics alive at any given time. These souls are said to represent the twelve apostles. When one stigmatic dies the gift is passed to someone new.

DH. *So Donna is a substitute. What religion forces a child's body, wincing and bleeding, into significance?*

MR. There's the child's volition in all of this, Daniel. To be honest with you, even I am a little confused. It's unlikely that an eleven-year-old girl would know enough about medieval stigmatics to mimic them, and yet in Donna's case, the mystical phenomena replicate those of the past. The blood flowing from an invisible wound, the presentation in the week before Easter, and the effect on the community.

DH. *How has this been received? I mean apart from newspaper reports and the rumour mill, Annex seems remarkably phlegmatic in its reception of what appears to be a miracle.*

MR. Who knows how these things may be received? Sometimes whole communities are thrown into a state of piety. Sometimes personality cults grow up around the stigmatic, rumours of miracles, claims of healing. In cases where whole communities have been caught up in this—this collective *spasm* of piety, more than one person may be carrying the marks. In these cases we must ask, is it the stigmatic who encourages group devotions? Or is the stigmatic merely the product of these waves of energy, these revivals of faith? In this case, since a child is involved, we can only be thankful that the fuss has died down.

DH. *To what do you attribute Donna's experience, Father Ricci? I mean in your opinion, what in the child elicits such grace?*

MR. Would you believe me if I said empathy? She has a quality of empathy, that child. . . . I had a parishioner once who witnessed her son being shot. The boy died and the mother—who was physically unharmed—began to develop a mark on her chest. Over the course of a week, the surface of the skin became increasingly painful, broke surface, began to seep blood. Do you see? The woman suffered from injuries she had not received but had witnessed in a beloved other. The wounds were not hers but his. However, are not all instances of the stigmata acts of empathy with the suffering of Christ?

DH. *And the Desjardins family?*

MR. I'll be frank with you, Daniel. I'm their protector, their spiritual counselor. The child has no earthly father, I'm responsible for her well-being, I have taken her confession. You, on the other hand, are a journalist—

DH. *I just want to know a little of the family. I haven't had much luck in reaching the mother. Would it be possible to arrange an interview?*

MR. Well, as for Donna, you must understand that so young a child cannot be allowed to speak to the Press. Donna has given no interviews, will not do so. But Mrs. Desjardins, well perhaps that can be arranged. For a fee. There is a fund set up at present, you see, to take care of expenses should Donna prove to be seriously ill. I'll contact you later on that account.

DH. *Thanks. Since you've been so obliging, I wonder if you could describe the family to me.*

MR. The father, Desjardins, was a miner from Québec. Mrs. Desjardins tells me he's dead, but I suspect he abandoned the family after the birth of the third child. They live on Railway Avenue. The house is comfortable, if a little crowded. A grandmother lives with them, you see, keeps house while the mother works as a cleaner at the hospital. The family are Sunday churchgoers, but until recently were unremarkable in matters of religion. There are three children, Adam is Donna's older brother. An advanced case of Down's syndrome, which is a cruel way of putting it, I know. Perhaps disease is his limit, as it is his sister's glory. Also, there is another child, a baby, the "youngest, smallest, thirdest," that is how the fairy tales put it. And then there is Donna.

DH. *And then there is Donna.*

MR. Oh brave new world that there should be such wonders! No, perhaps the wonder is all on my part. Donna is—Donna is not unlike her schoolmates. Quieter perhaps, more sensitive than most, certainly. Otherwise just a normal child. She eats her ice-cream in three hungry-girl bites, then throws the cone away. You see, this is how I too know I've grown up—these days I lick carefully around the edges. With the tip of my tongue I push the ice-cream back into the cone! Donna, now. . . . Five years ago when they first moved to this town Mrs. Desjardins came to see me. It seems that her daughter was to be found talking often with a little friend. Nothing wrong with that, except the friend in question had been killed in a drowning accident up at Leaf Rapids. I did not find this kind of behaviour inconsistent with grief and persuaded her mother to pass over it unremarked. Indeed, the activity did in fact fade over time and the friend has not been mentioned these last four years.

DH. *So she's what you'd describe as a well-adjusted child?*

MR. Well-adjusted, yes. And, please God, will remain so. After all, the Bible teaches that as it is written, so it will be done. Let's hope so.

———— End of Transcript ————

Gentle Reader,

As it is written, so it is done. Amen to that. It
was hot today, the hottest day of the year so far, 32.5 degrees
even under the trees; poplar, maple, birch. I've sat all day
in this close house, reading through the transcripts Daniel
Halpern left. Regina came in once to place a vase of freshly
picked rosebuds at my elbow. They reminded me of bloodied
swabs, the small pink pout of too soon blooms, and when
she left, I removed them to the kitchen window-sill. The coffee
in my mouth is bitter and nostalgic. I am remembering the
girl l was the first and only time I left this house.

Poor Robert Dunning, or Farmer Bob, as he was called. We are
nothing if not a literal people. Perhaps that was the problem—
my figurative tendencies, my horror of the self-evident, my
impatience with horizons, boredom, conversations about the
weather, and the whole sweaty, messy, reductive enterprise of
jam-making. Imagine a woman who reads, who writes more

than she lives. All she can think of is short-circuiting the household chores, escaping to her blank white mind, her books, her
sheets of yellow legal pad, her pencils freshly sharpened and
smelling of cedar wood. When her husband comes home from
the fields, the dinner is barely ready, there is a flurry to peel
potatoes, brown meat. She knows he deserves something better
than these acrostic moments between *hi honey* and *night dear*.
If you ask her she'll say she loves him, say he is the rock upon
which she is cleft. Say marriage is a series of slowly widening
compromises, the difference between *then* and *now* is a dash of
butter and a sprinkling of salt.

Well, so much for that woman. We arrive now at a logistical
problem: Virginie Waters. She needs to be introduced, without
premeditation. Let me see now, Virginie. . . . She is a woman
who writes beautiful letters, indeed she is much better on paper
than in person. Last year when she went to spend Christmas
in Montréal, she sent me a postcard. *My dear, just a note to tell
you that I miss you (and so, I miss you)*. The sentimental grease
of the first statement cut by the lemon-scented stringency of the
second. Of course, the effect was also to distance emotion. If
I miss you, she implies, it is only in parenthesis: life, my life,
goes on beyond the cultivated phrase.

When she came to this town from the east, she was an anachronistic figure. Stylish, her hair cut on the bias, she moved with intimidating precision through this untidy town. A subject of predictable curiosity, she nevertheless fulfilled a purpose, taking over her father's position and ministering to his assorted patients. Of course there is ceaseless speculation as to why she came to this place. Popular opinion has a man involved, but since none have come forward, and her personal life is chaste in the extreme, this has proved a threadbare theory. My own feeling is simply that she is tired. Imagine the body as an hourglass: each woman has a finite number of breaths to breathe, words to speak, ripe kisses to fall from her lips. Now, imagine a body stuffed with sand, leaking sawdust. It is my opinion that Virginie Waters has come to the end of what she believes are her body's natural resources. In her, the image and the imprint can no longer be imagined separately.

And yes, there is someone at the bottom of her flight, not here but there. The one she moved halfway across the country to leave, poor girl. For her, love is an affliction. Only pain bears witness to her experience. Poor girl, poor baby, you might say. Of course, this is all speculation on my part, Virginie has not taken me into her confidence, nor do l imagine that she will. She is a fine and private citizen, nothing at all like her father the doctor, who, if you have not guessed by now, was a particular friend of mine. She has his eyes, you know, that thick shade of blue that resembles the lining of a song about velvet.

When I was younger I wanted to be loved madly, irrationally, without logic. I wanted to wound with my silence, with my lack of attention, my slow withdrawal like a glass of water swallowed, drop by drop. All I recall now, sharp as hangnail memory, is the allusive colour of the new doctor's eyes. It is difficult to escape cliché in matters of the body, we have only so many orifices that secrete, so many extremities that harden, so many sounds that can be forced from our pliant mouths.

When Virginie's mother left her home and her husband and took her daughter to Montréal, the doctor and I assumed an intimacy that would, we hoped, cure us both of old ghosts, bury them deep and salt the ground in which they lay. After all, like his absent wife, I was a woman who had left her marriage to return to her first home. In me he hoped to crack the code that had opened his life wide to loss. For my part, I felt safe with him because he was familiar, almost a member of the family.

We are all blue-eyed in my family, so perhaps the world is tinted that way too. At the edges, like the thin breath of skim milk. Perhaps blue is the eye of my beholding, another word for melancholy, a thing at once tender and corrupt, the better part of depression. A tidal sort of emotion with deep breaths in between, the opposite of fretful. Like the air you breathe out on one of those rotten days in late fall, everything mortal in the balance; hands and feet, pears hanging from branches. And time inverted, years falling like scales.

He liked to turn me over in my sleep and rearrange me, hand over hand. Then he'd pull me up to him by the neck as if I were a kitten. On those rare mornings when we'd wake together in one bed, he'd reach over, say *little one*, little one, what are you singing? Are you happy today? His death did not coincide with the end of our relationship, but for all that I was oddly happy. He demanded so little; a home-cooked meal every other week, chicken pot-pie and an exaggerated soufflé on Sundays. Beneath the ministrations of his warm mouth, my body grew labile, pliant. Quite suddenly my breasts began to grow, swelled defiantly, split careful neck buttons apart, spoilt the line of shirtwaists. My nipples that had always been classic and pink, darkened to the colour of old pennies.

Virginie, now. I wouldn't be surprised if she knew nothing of my connection to her father. They had very little to do with one another when she was a child. Her mother was a brackish woman with an ingrown soul. It's unlikely that she would have spoken to the daughter about her father. Now it's my sheer good fortune to have her so near, for in the turn of her head, in her broad, good-natured hands, I glimpse his familiar.

Virginie. *In the middle of my life I woke in a dark wood.* Like Dante's traveller, she has come to this small town. Despair yea. Virginie, child, I want to say, your father did not kill himself for love of you, for love of me. He was the one who left us in the end, nothing we have done anticipated his reply. That she has come to work here as a form of penance does not worry me as much as the fact that she expects enlightenment to proceed from penance, truth to rise to the surface, buoyant as a corpse on the salt licks of our shored-up sins. I watch her each night as she sits in the window of the log cabin, writing letters, making curt notes in her journal.

Some evenings I lure her to my kitchen with the promise of information, pour tea, cut scones, offer her sugar, cream, along with the two or three things I know about him. That he had kind hands, that he was a good doctor, that his breath smelt of wintergreen and spilt whiskey. That he knew something of the medieval history of flowers, that he spoke, like God, in the first person. That he believed in a conspiracy of interiors, the night's stored sadness rushing out at him when he unlocked his office door in the morning. That towards the end, his ribs floated to the surface of his skin. That he loved you, Virginie. Oh, and we know how he died. We never speak of how he died.

The last thing he said to me was *I'm not sure if I'm doing the most courageous thing I've ever done in my life, or the most cowardly.* I said, forgive me for having my own opinion on the matter. He put his head down to mine like some great, sad lion about to drink from a pond. We did not touch.

In my need to remember him the way I used to, with *tendresse,* I imagine that he is alive, that I telephone him late at night, wake him from tumbled sheets and a going-going-gone dream. *Hello.* Maybe in that one word get back to the thin slice of him I once had. But already he's waking, his voice has changed gear, he's getting ready to blow jokes like bubbles. Goodbye, I say, *click.*

He died three days before Christmas. That same night there was a fire in a Winnipeg factory that manufactured Christmas decorations. Imagine all that tinsel flaring, angels with their painted cheeks and heavenswept eyes turning transparent, crumpling to ash. The glass balls, coloured lights, giving in to their electrical impulses, a series of innumerable small pops beneath the deep orange snapcrackle tide. And the stars set to blaze, blazing. A movement across verbs. The workers at their stations sunk into that quiet night, their agitated hands the last things to lapse silent. And afterwards, the shook foil of the night centred upon newsprint.

My sweet Ginny, how she is troubled by endings that fail to
rhyme. She tells me she has come to this place to forget one
man and to remember another. She tells me she sleeps deeply,
dreamlessly. I imagine her asleep in the log cabin. A land
animal at sea, she breaks surface, her slow heart pumping
blubber. In her sleep she walks the streets of another city. For
Ginny, home is the place you know like the back of your hand,
the palmed map. And coming home involves all manner of
detours to produce the truths she requires.

She is considered a welcome addition to the town. We are all
predisposed to like her, and make much of her, since her father
was valued, even the circumstances of an unorthodox death
forgiven in the wake of his tonsured life. More to the point, she
is someone to whom general approval is rendered, a chaste-
looking woman not prone to appetite or exaggeration, her
hospital whites entirely unsuggestive. Mina Isaacs, whom I visit
often at the Care Home, calls her an *angel*, but Mina is without
irony. Yet, it's no small matter to be universally respected. Even
that exasperating hedonist, Father Ricci, has failed to tempt
Virginie away from herself. He visited her the other day, I saw
his white escort pull up beside the cabin, but he left when he
failed to get a response to his officious knock. Before he got
back into the car I saw him stoop and place a parcel against
her door. What a fool that man is, with his piety and his letters

to the archbishop and his unforgivably plump haunches!

Outside this window I see Regina disappearing into the prairie grass on the farthest outskirts of my property. She carries a pair of secateurs and looks altogether too set upon her unbewildered course. We have been avoiding each other all day, our bodies insistent, narrative. We should not be having these misunderstandings, I said to her, we're not lovers! I have set myself the task of re-reading Proust, almost entirely to avoid speaking to her. With the taste of a Madeleine dissolving nostalgically on my tongue I glance outside. It's windy and she appears to be laughing high and hard to herself. I know what she's up to, just as I know that my disapproval can only serve to goad her on.

The wild flowers in this country are not for the picking, they instantly wilt along their stems. There is a particular variety of buttercup I have looked for all my life, only papa has seen it. When I find this flower I will not suffer it to be stuffed into a vase or pressed between the pages of a book. When I find it at last, I will kneel to it, the articulation of butter.

As for Virginie, she does not have the temperament for redemption. That she is good, *intensely* good, full of moral rectitude, is beyond question. But virtue is not a word we bring up in polite conversation these days. It is at once too suggestive of

whatever it is that our town lacks, and the lengths we would
have to go to circumvent our own beliefs. Virginie, with her
ascerbic half-smile, has had to learn to imprint herself on the
oblique surfaces of this world. Like all of us, her hands blacken
with newsprint, her forearms turn crisp in the sun, her fingertips wrinkle to walnut halves in the bath.

The only thing she has not yet learned is to allow the inexplicable to dissolve in her bloodstream like aspirin. Unlike the
rest of us who have fashioned what is miraculous into a reason-
able facsimile of the everyday, she is truly distraught by what
she persists in calling Donna's pathology. More than this,
the Desjardins girl seems to have laid claim to whatever is in
Ginny that kneels before God or love, truth, beauty or pity.
I sense in her this need to immolate herself before something
greater than individual will, and it is precisely this cravenness
that I will not lightly forgive, should my forgiveness ever be
required. Aah Halpern, what a pair you two would have made,
the one running away, the other towards, some unrepeatable
version of the wingéd soul.

The wind today was like a consumptive hand reaching into
my lungs and scooping them out, and no, I've never been ill
a day in my life. I will admit at last to a concise passion of my
own. I have a thirst—*like Tantalus*, as father would say—for

other people's business. Sifting through Halpern's transcripts these last few days has not in any way slaked my need to know what it is my gentle neighbour is so busy writing up in those perverse journals of hers. But Virginie is not Halpern, she is no writer and so not susceptible to the lure of the reader. I can see that my only entrance into her writing may well be through my own. That *imagination* rather than knowledge will have to suffice in this instance.

Virginie Waters' Journal

Friday, 21 April.

Saw Adam Desjardins, Donna's older brother, in town today. I went into Ruhudsky's Supplies to buy a stopper for the door and there he was sitting on a bale of twine, an oddly virile figure amongst the balls of wire and copper, the shelves stacked with power tools and nails in assorted sizes, the smell of fresh-cut pine. Crouched down on his barrel, with the terraced forehead of the mongoloid adolescent, his eyes were large and deep-set, seeming to absorb rather than reflect light.

    Geisler took me to the back of the store where he keeps the brass-ware and when we came back Adam had the fly of his pants open and was manipulating a large and unquestionably erect penis with the fingers of his right hand. It looked like he was pretending to change gears, pulling it backwards and forwards and to the left with a sound he made deep in his throat, a surprisingly accurate facsimile of a motor car moving up a steep incline. Geisler threw him out but I got the impression that this was neither an unexpected nor an especially *shocking event, and that the eviction was for my benefit.*

When I got home I saw that someone had left a small brown parcel inside my screen door. From Father Massimo, the note read, hoping that recent events have dispelled doubts. I expect he was referring, with priestly alliteration, to the business with Donna, because inside was an odd little volume rather pompously entitled, The Book of Bella-Marie Lambe: The Life of a Saint. Something in the note or the gift annoyed me and I pushed it away into a corner of my desk. For want of anything more corporeal to berate, I began to beat up a couple of eggs for my supper.

Monday, 24 April.

Strange patient today, Regina Arnott. I've seen her before, buying groceries at the Foodtown, and once I saw her come out of the bar at the Number Eight when I was driving into town for a delivery. It was very late and very cold, I knew she shouldn't be out alone and probably drunk but it was a breach birth and I couldn't stop. Anyway, she's never consulted me before but she said immediately, I knew the old doctor, your father. She never said anything further, not like his other patients who could spend hours if I would let them, praising his dedication, his presence of mind in an emergency, his gentle hands. No, it was not praise she had in mind. Like me, she had come to bury Caesar.

She was consulting me about something quite negligible, an

ingrown toenail that was neither uncomfortable nor infected, and
I got the impression she was looking me over. For a moment her
watchfulness reminded me of a patient I once had, an Iranian who'd
been tortured in prison by having the soles of his feet beaten. Although
his feet were badly disfigured, a mass of scar tissue and cicatriced
ridges, he no longer felt pain in them at all. Instead, he told me that
during the beatings he had suffered from agonizing pain in different
parts of his body. Never the feet, but corresponding instead to the
foot's reflexes.

Regina sat before me with her coarse man's sock in her hand, her
barefoot toes strong and splayed, like taproots. She began to tell me a
strange, rambling story about a woman who came to her because she
couldn't fall pregnant. I gather Regina is a kind of faith-healer in the
town and that people come to her for home remedies and cures for
sterility and impotence.

What advice did you give her? I asked.

I told her to massage his testicles like they were milkteats on a
cow. She was laughing, a guttural sound from the deep of her belly.
That's what my mother had to do to get me!

I joined in her laughter and then, because it was a slow day at
the clinic, I asked her about her family. At first she seemed to resent
the question and began to draw on her sock, then suddenly she bent
towards me and began to laugh again, but all she would say was, Oh,
I grew up in an ecstatic kind of family!

There was a smell like loam off her breath.

Wednesday, 26 April.

*Just back from seeing Molly Rhutabaga. When I came home from
work this evening there was a branch of pussy-willow tied to my door
handle and a square of notepaper trimmed with robins inviting me to
tea. She often makes these careful, delicate gestures towards me, even
though the distance between my cabin and her house is only a shout
away. She has the charming, old-fashioned belief that telephones
are intrusive, like voices breaking contemplative space. Also, I think
she knows something of quiet, the need I have these days of long slow
dusks, an auctioned silence.*

*Anyway, we had tea in her square green kitchen. She set the table
with cabbage rose china teacups on a handworked cloth, and there
were cheese biscuits and slices of apple and pear sprinkled with lemon
juice to prevent browning, and small pats of jam and butter, and a
glass dish of shortbread. You must miss your family terribly, my dear,
she said, pouring my tea. Underneath the table the dog stirred, shifted.
The tea was properly made with loose leaves, a teapot and warmer.
No, I answered truthfully, I feel as if they're with me wherever I am.
She nodded wisely. Aah well, you're still young, my dear.*

*I asked her about Regina Arnott and she nodded her head
decidedly, pursed her mouth and said, she always gives me old
chocolates, broken jewelry and wilted flowers—she's magic and she's
bad. But she offset this remark with laughter, as if she were paying
her a great compliment.*

We talked about what she called, the young man from the news-

paper. She seemed to think that Halpern is more serious than the others, less ignorant, as she put it, by which she intends a subtle range of meanings beginning with respectful and ending with honest.

I know very little about him, I told her, which strikes me as odd now that I think of it. She saw him at the Foodtown and liked the cut of his jib. Her words. I imagine the dark serviceable cloth of Halpern's jib. About him something of the deliberation of a comb finding its way through wet hair.

Sunday, 30 April.

Two years ago today, I woke up crying because I could see all the days of pain before me like a long staircase going neither up nor down. I got out of bed and made myself a slice of anchovy toast and took out the goose-down quilt because what the hell, bodies can be made a little more comfortable. Last night on television someone's lover left him, o h g o d, i t h u r t s he said, and burst into tears. It was some dreary sit-com or other, and the joke is this man crying and no-one wanting to comfort him. Love gone wrong is shameful, I think, even in the movies.

We used to fight about the TV, but not really. By which I mean that the hostilities were real if poorly motivated. He wanted to watch the news, I wanted to read. Once during a fight he took hold of me and hugged me so tightly I felt the imprint of his bones against my flesh. His body was resistant, bright, with I'm not sure what emotion. Anger and resentment are two of my guesses.

I began to think about endings, which for me have always been sudden, unannounced. One night I woke up, he was leaning on one arm, staring down at me. You're so pretty asleep, he said, you smell so good, I can't touch you. He looked regretful and resolved at the same time, the beginning of what I would one day be obliged to call the end.

What was so sad is that I started to hope he would notice me again and all I saw in his eyes was the awareness that my hair was windblown or my earrings crooked. We stood in the apricot afternoon beside the wrought iron steps of our apartment. He faced me, leaning against the back of a car. Suddenly the Montréal streets were full of dragonflies and cats. While we stood there a cat did a backflip to catch a dragonfly in her naughty mouth. There was a scalding place, the size of a steam-iron, above my diaphragm. My hair was windblown, my earrings crooked.

When I first came to Annex I used to take long walks in the evenings. For exercise, I told myself, to walk off the sedentary life. But it was really just my moth-nature. At a certain time of the evening there was a just-fallen rather than an already-drawn darkness, the living room lights on in all the houses and if the curtains were not tightly closed, I could see the families getting ready for their evening, children watching television, food heating on the stove. I would like to say I was less lonely with him.

What does it mean to wait? The image of a window springs to mind. Sweet Marianne who would rather be dead, plucky Penelope unhemming her accumulated life. Far away a horseman gallops over the horizon, the Lady of Shallot looks aghast, he has come, but much too early. Think of the breathlessness of chairs in waiting rooms, doctor's offices, bingo halls, church pews. What else? A clock, the asymptomatic ring of the telephone, the breath before speech you recognize on the other side of the line.

Waiting rehearses disruption, anticipates the moment after. Until then, nothing is very absorbing. You switch television channels listlessly, turn down the corner of a book, take a bath, page through fashion magazines. Perhaps something to eat? A bite of something salty has its own impetus—now you require a glass of water.

For waiting I would recommend small bites of things nutty, spicy, difficult to chew. Try breadsticks, sunflower seeds, small resilient carrots, hard biscuits. Avoid the sweet, the soft, the overly accommo-dating flesh of pastry or pie. The tooth needs something against which to resist. Nuts, in their perversely packaged shells, are particularly helpful. I myself take great comfort in pistachios.

Two years ago pain was the cold metal barometer that kept me upright and in this world, the mercury shooting through my body in quicksilver spurts. I woke up every morning, began to breathe, opened my lungs as wide as the sky. Only the sun was constant, an asymmetrical eye above me. Every day I got out of bed, made myself a sandwich for lunch, washed apples. The thought of talking to people about anything not related to their ill-health and my expertise made me weep. All the same, however bad it got, I knew it would pass.

I have enormous faith in my powers of resilience. Nowadays I don't even turn away at the sight of lovers!

Monday, 1 May.
Even when I am in Montréal, I long for Montréal.

Tuesday, 2 May.
This morning, woke up tossed between wet sheets, the mattress bare, my hands clenched. It's not sexual release I want, that moment when you lose language, unless Jesus and God and oh Christ! count, verbs I mean, and descriptive nouns and connectives.

Couldn't sleep last night so I took out the book Father Ricci lent me. An oddly heavy object, The Book of Bella-Marie Lambe: The Life of a Saint. It is stamped in gold-print on blue leather and the pages are foxed, here and there, by time or ill-use. It seems to be a kind of vita nuova, like the sisters were so fond of reading, written by a surgeon with the name of Thomas Honeycombe. In the prologue he fatuously describes himself as, "a Collector of Somatic Miracles as well as the Writer of a Treatise on Gynecology." He appears to be inordinately concerned with what goes on in the bodies of women!

Bella-Marie Lambe was a novice, a nunlet, as we used to call them, in a convent in the north of England at the end of the fourteenth century. The good doctor Honeycombe writes in 1395, the story of her passion and beatification told largely from his rotund perspective. It

seems that during an Easter Mass she was visited by a vision of Christ,
who told her, and I quote; "You are like a grape, ripe. When you are
crushed, that juice refreshes me; I am thirsty for souls." At which point
she began to bleed profusely from her palms and the soles of her feet.
One of the nuns present at the stigmatization witnessed that the blood,
"ran up and over the altar and into the chalice so that it was soon
filled and o'er brimming."

I stopped reading at this point, angry at that fat priest's
presumption. Ricci, I mean and not whoever it was took charge of poor
Bella-Marie. As I was closing the book, a page fell open to a poem by
Lambe, written after a vision. It was coldly beautiful, a chilled set of
verses about Divine Love entitled The Desert Has Twelve
Things. *I copied the first verse because it expresses everything I no*
longer care to about love and its misalliances.

> *You must love nothingness,*
> *You must flee something,*
> *You must remain alone*
> *And go to nobody.*

Wednesday, 3 May.
* He said I didn't miss you.
* He threw teacups across the room, pulled telephones from the wall,
  put his fists through windows, doors, dry-wall.
* He said I hate you I hate you, in cars, in parking lots, on
  cold snow days.

* *He gave me his pain to hatch.*
* *He dismantled me with his hands.*
* *He made me come, past all coming.*
* *He said I've always hated you, in cars, on mountain roads, in early spring.*
* *He left his fingerprints on my collarbone.*
* *He said I'll never hurt you, comma, never.*

Thursday, 4 May.
Even when I was with you, I longed for you.

Friday, 5 May.
Had my second follow-up session with Donna Desjardins today. Something about that child worries me. Her mother brought her in but didn't stay, as she had a job to finish up in ward three. She'll just sit in the waiting room when you're finished with her, she told me, I get off at five and she's a good girl.

Donna sat upright against the back of her chair, very straight, her feet not quite touching the ground. She answered all my questions clearly and without guile, as she has always. No, the bleeding has stopped, yes, school is back to normal, yes, the other kids have stopped teasing her. I asked about her home life, her grandmother, the baby. She shrugged her shoulders, spindrift bones moving awkwardly beneath her thick sweater, then told me her brother's not going to school anymore.

Her brother used to attend the local elementary school as a special student, until the only volunteer went on maternity leave and the teachers found they couldn't attend to him. Mum says he's too big for school, but I think it's because he shows the girls his pee-pee, she said.

What does he do? I asked. He stays at home, she told me, helps their grandmother. Suddenly she had a story, and the blood moved more quickly beneath her skin, her cheekbones flushed. Last summer their grandmother set him to catching all the snails in their garden. She provided him with a bucket and a shaker to salt them down. Then she and Donna went into town to do their grocery shopping. When they came back the front of the house was crawling with snails, snails were inching their way vertically up to the second storey, leaving a trail of fine slime on the windows. The grandmother flew into a rage and hit out at Adam but Donna had seen something in the apparently random pattern of the snails against the wall. A giant if lopsided "A." Her brother had been trying to spell his name, she concluded, but there weren't enough snails.

It's late now, the light in Molly's kitchen window has gone out and I feel strangely lonely without that curt rectangle against the darkness. If it were still light out she would be walking across the garden, leaving wet footprints in the rotting snow. She would be wearing her old gardening coat and gloves, her hair tied with a scarf, and carrying a shovel or a length of fencing. Then, if I were sitting here, she would turn around, catch my eye and wave. That terrier of

hers, *Franklin* she calls him, would jump up and down and I'd see his
tail wagging and his jaws moving but no sound can penetrate these
storm windows. I don't know why she is so important to me. Perhaps
I think that by watching her I can learn to grow old.

Had a strange and detailed dream last night, I remembered it
quite suddenly while preparing Mr. Hruniak's catheter. I was walking
through the rooms of a gallery in Montréal, an exhibition of
Babylonian artifacts. I remember standing in front of a circumcision
set composed of an ivory half-egg on a silver stand, presumably to take
the flap of skin away, and what looked like a fruit-paring knife with
a bone inlaid handle. Next to this was a stone osiary with these words
inscribed on its side: *my father spoke to me thus before
he died; first bury my body in the ground then
place my bones in an osiary.*

That would be just like a father, wouldn't it! Bury my body,
dig me up, then bury it again. In other words, *remember me,
Hamlet.* As for my own father, he remains dead, although I have
travelled halfway across the country to agitate his bones.

Saturday, 6 May.
Been seeing my father everywhere these days. First playing bank
robbers in an old movie, shooting up some midwestern town in the
upturned bowl of the Depression. Then in a graphic advertisement for
hair loss as I was flicking to the weather channel. And lately on the
street in front of me. After the first glance, there is no other. His image

rattles to coin in the begging bowl of my imaginative need. Always I
am reminded of that last good-bye when the airplane moved diagonally
into the sky and our bodies turned quite naturally, as on a pivot.

I remember sitting at the waterfront with my mother, eating
sandwiches, the wind kept blowing her hair into her mouth. The sun
had begun to travel down the outside of the spice warehouses in front
of us. It had already reached the second storey and in my memory, the
mingled scents of saffron and cumin began to stain the afternoon
sepia. Shrugging her eloquent shoulders, my mother said, You fall in
love with someone and then you get married—it's not as easy as it
sounds. Autumn had begun to set small fires in the maples around us,
a drift of leaves floated to our feet. They fell freely, neither i n l o v e
nor f r o m g r a c e.

C o m e   b a c k   p a p a, I want to call at these times, I d o n ' t
k n o w   y o u. Through the contrivance of my mother he is carefully
absent from the photograph albums, the letters, the family names. Gone
from the alphabets, the family Bible, the library books. Here is a list
of things I have not yet seen in this country:

* the beaver whose teeth marks Molly showed me on the reed she
  brought back from the river.
* the shooting star Geisler pointed to last Saturday night when we
  went out to look at the sky, his breath smoky with dark rum.
* the deer Molly insists walks regularly through the undergrowth at
  sunset, her ears fanning the wind.

Sunday, 7 May.

Just got back from the hospital, it seems the whole town is in an uproar again. I got an emergency call on my beeper and when I arrived at the hospital, Regina Arnott was waiting for me. Someone had covered her with a blanket but she was shaking violently and the cotton was soaked with her blood. Father Ricci had brought her in. He told me she was attending a mass when she suddenly began to bleed copiously, sensationally, all over the altar. He seemed shaken and a little frightened. I suspect that, after all, the miraculous is messier than he has been led to expect.

My own reaction was one of outrage. I didn't know I could see a thing and still not believe I was seeing it. Perhaps it's time for another look at that blessed Saint's Life after all.

THE BOOK OF BELLA-MARIE LAMBE:
THE LIFE OF A SAINT
As Confessed to and Inscribed by Father Thomas
Honeycombe, Surgeon at the Court of His Majesty the King.

✠ Here begins a short treatise and a comforting one for sinful wretches, in which they may find great solace and comfort for themselves, and understand the high and unspeakable mercy of our sovereign Saviour Jesus Christ—whose name be worshipped and magnified without end. And for all those who have faith and trust, or shall have faith and trust, grace as they desire, spiritual or bodily to the profit of their souls, I pray you Lord, grant them, from the abundance of your mercy, amen.

When this creature was but twelve years old, her father died and she was betrothed to a young man from a neighboring estate who died but three short years thereafter, and in her grief and sore distress, Bella-Marie Lambe entered the convent at Basel much to the sadness of her family. And when this creature had thus, through grace, come again to her right mind, she thought she was bound to God and that she would be His servant.

Nevertheless, she would not leave behind her pride in her showy manner of dressing, which she had previously been used to, wearing gold piping on her head and hoods with tippets that were fashionably slashed. Even in the convent at Basel she wore cloaks that were modishly slashed and underlaid with various colours between the slashes, so that she would be all the more stared at, and all the more esteemed.

In the Easter of her second year, this creature underwent a vision during mass wherein she found herself to be kneeling at the cross, and while she swooned with Love over the body of Our Lord that writhed and bled before her, she flowered like a tree in Spring and her verdant branches were labeled with the names of the Five Senses. And as those who love Christ should respond to all of His body with all of theirs, this creature was strengthened in heart by the Holy Bread, inebriated in mind by the Holy Wine. And as the holy body fattened her, the vitalizing blood purified her, sometimes as a taste of honey, sometimes as a sweet smell, and sometimes in the pure and gorgeously embellished marriage bed of the heart.

And when the Mass was over she remained prone before the altar, her sisters could not persuade her to rise. Indeed since her lids remained closed and her flesh was unnaturally pallid, she seemed to witnesses to be fast approaching that chasm between this life and the next.

But she awakened in due course and immediately requested a taste again of that sweet sacrament since she could not bear to abstain from such solace for long. And still she was not able to bear any longer her thirst for the vivifying blood, and when she was refused, for the Mass at Basel occurs but once a day and then at evening, she remained a long time on her knees before the altar contemplating the empty chalice.

And thus she told her confessor, that it was the same for her to live as to eat the body of Christ, and to be separated from the sacrament was to die without savour of sweetness or hope. This she felt not only in her soul but also in her mouth. And like Dorothy of Montane before her, she soon became frantic without the sacrament and fought her confessor for a taste of the holy bread.

Herewith immediately follows a list of the Miracles that this creature, Bella-Marie Lambe underwent in her pursuit of the Eucharist:

✢ A Miracle in which the Recipient becomes a crystal filled with Light.

✢ A Miracle in which the Recipient distinguishes between the consecrated and the unconsecrated Host.

✢ A Miracle in which the Recipient feels the Eucharist to Act upon her Senses as when the mouth fills with honey and so forth.

✢ A Miracle in which the Recipient perceives the host or the chalice to transform into an infant.

✢ A Miracle in which the Recipient is observed to live entirely on the host as her only food and substance.

✢ A Miracle in which the Recipient perceives herself to be a supplicant in the presence of Christ who offers himself as food by tearing flesh from his breast, palms, and so forth.

For the first two years when this creature was thus drawn to our Lord she had great quiet of spirit from any temptations. Then it was she talked to her confessor thus:

> Jesus made of his blood a drink and his flesh a food for all those who wish it. There is no other means to satisfy hunger and thirst. When upon the cross His heart was lanced open, the Holy Spirit tells us to have recourse to the blood. And then the soul becomes like a drunken man; the more he drinks, the more he wants to drink. And the pain is its refreshment and the tears which it has shed for the memory of the blood are its drink. And the sighs are its food.

At this time she also received permission for daily communion, for it was painful for her to be in exile from the host, so painful that she had stormed the altar of the church to get at the pyx. But soon she had no further need for these duplicities because she was able to eat her Lord at will by reciting John 1.14. For whenever she spoke the words *Verbum caro factum est,* which she was in the habit of inserting into the Hours whenever possible, she tasted the Word on her tongue and felt flesh in her mouth which she chewed, distilling from it the aftertaste of honey. Thus this woman of great and profound virility saw in Christ the incarnated God, a subject who is the life of the flesh, both creator and creature, Christ as Infant, as Bridegroom, as tortured Body on the Cross.

On one occasion, when this creature journeyed to Canterbury, she was greatly despised by the Monks and reproved by the Priests because she wept so much—all morning and all evening in fact—and when she was not weeping she told stories from scripture. Then it was that a Monk said to her, "Either you have the Holy Ghost or else you have a devil within you, for what you are speaking here to us is Holy Writ, and that you do not have of yourself."

Also it was at this time that this creature received a vision while she lay at prayer, in which a dish completely filled with carved-up flesh was offered to her while the voice of God identified this flesh as that of Christ and warned that it was human sin that had minced His son into such small pieces.

There followed a series of miracles in which the bread turned back into bloody flesh in the mouth of this creature. She spoke at this time of her love for Christ, which followed upon an inestimable satiety, *"which although it satiates, generates at the same time insatiable hunger, so that all of my members are unstrung."*

This creature was sent by our Lord to diverse places of religion, and amongst them she came to a place of Monks where she was despised, for these Monks not only set no value on her at all, but held her to be a displeasure. For it was at this time that she began to reject the Eucharist wafer offered her by the Priest, insisting that she had her own and that it came directly from Christ. This was judged to be an offense against God and she was gnawed by the people of the world just as any rat gnaws the stockfish, so that it seemed to her that she had taken the hair-shirt off her back and placed it upon her heart. It was said of her that she claimed clerical power for herself, a woman, and in so doing usurped priestly authority.

It came to her at this time that human suffering can join the reservoir of suffering that is purgatory, and that the Soul is a noble creature blackened by the flesh which can nevertheless be exalted by hunger, thirst and beatings. Wailing miserably, she began to beat her breast and her body: *"O miserable and wretched body! How long will you torment me? O miserable soul! Why are you scorning me in this way?"*

After this vision, she resolved to do great bodily penance. She was shriven two or three times a day and gave herself up to much fasting and keeping of vigils. Three times a night she rose at the hour of the clock and went to the church where she remained at her prayers until midday. Still she was much reproved and slandered by many because she led so strict a life.

Here follows, furthermore, an account of women who have chosen to suffer for Our Lord, written down here for convenience, inasmuch as it is like those matters that have been written before, notwithstanding that they happened long before the matters that follow.

✝ As item; Beatrice of Ornacieux who thrust a nail completely through her hand in imitation of our Lord, but only clear water flowed from the wound.

✝ As item; Mary of Oignies who cut off pieces of her own flesh, then buried them in the ground to keep from her confessor the secret of what she had done.

✝ As item; Angela of Foligno who sucked the scabs from the wounds of lepers and found them as sweet as communion.

Thus Bella-Marie Lambe of the convent of Our Lady at Basel resolved to embrace her pain as a source of grace, proclaiming *"Lord wound me with the wound of love which may be healed only by being wounded!"* And so saying she thrust nettles between her breasts, donned a hair-cloth, the kind upon which malt is dried, and walked barefoot into the desert, praying with great love and bitterness, and performing thousands of genuflections.

Many weeks passed, but when the time came for the creature to return she was not able to rise to her feet, as she had weakened during this time from fasting, but also from great love. Then it was that God filled her dry virgin breasts with milk and she was able to nurse herself and rise and walk upon the hot sand saying, *"I have been so poor that I have had nothing to renounce for God but food and even that he would not accept from me."*

After our Sovereign Saviour had taken her to his manifold mercy in this manner, she was able to communicate to her confessor the following vision:

My sweet Lord, you come to me as my mother. For
when the hour of your delivery came you were
placed on the hard bed of the cross, and your nerves
and all your bones were broken. And truly it is no
surprise that your veins burst when in one day you
gave birth to the whole world. For you took my
soul which was sensual, and united it to my sub-
stance, which was fleeting, a thing of this world.
Our Saviour is my true mother, in whom I am end-
lessly born, out of whom I shall ever come.

And she said, the Holy Church is our mother because she cares
for and nurtures us and Mary the Virgin is even more our mother
because she bore Christ. But Christ is mother most of all.

It was also at this time that she took to her heart this
text from the Song of Songs, *Come to me, beloved friends, and eat my*
flesh. Come to me, most beloved, in the cellar of wine and inebriate yourself
with my blood. And she would stand for many hours at a time
before the altarpiece upon which was rendered a *Lamentation of*
the Holy Trinity, and she would say, "*Not only was Christ enfleshed*
with flesh from a woman but see how his own flesh does womanly things,
how it bleeds, how it bleeds food, how it gives birth."

For the painting, by one Master Jean Malouel, called
attention to the blood which flowed from Christ's own breast
and into his crotch in defiance of the earth's magnetism and
as a reminder of the earlier wound of circumcision. And she
would look up to this picture, point, and say, "*Lo, how the blood*
purls from His wound. As Mary once fed her infant child now Christ
fills cups for his followers. It is from His nipples that the blood of the
Eucharist flows."

The priest who wrote down this book, in order to

test this creature's feelings, asked her many questions and bid her explain to him truly and without any pretending, how she felt, or else he would not have gladly written the book. And so this creature, partly compelled by the fear that he would not otherwise have completed her intention in writing this book, did as he asked her. And she told him, addressing him as Good Master Thomas and so forth, that to receive Christ's body in the ceremony of the host was for her to become Christ, insofar as Christ's flesh was her own, sealed within her womb like hot wax by the Holy Spirit.

What follows hereafter is an account of the Theory of Conception, whereby this Priest and also Surgeon of the Royal Academy of Physician's and Surgeons, cogitates upon the inner workings of the body of the woman when she is with child. As for the mother, she provides the matter of the fetus, as for the father, its form or spirit. In providing the unformed physical stuff of which the fully human is made, she is the oven or vessel, as Galen has said, in which the fetus cooks, and her body feeds the growing child with blood that transmutes when twice-cooked, into breast milk.

And furthermore that the apparatus of generation in women is like the apparatus of generation in men except that it is reversed. Indeed, a woman can turn into a man, if owing to an accident, the internal organs are suddenly pushed outward. For both the man and the woman, the shedding of excessive liquids is purgative and necessary, whether they be menstruative, lactative, seminal or hemorrhoidal, for the washing away of superfluity. What is not as easily explained is the inner working of the female saint's body that turns into a relic even before her death and in which the reception of such as the Eucharist leads naturally to the physical experience of the wounds of Christ's death by execution, that we have called *stigmata*.

On Corpus Christi Day, as the priests bore the sacrament about the town in procession, with many candles as was worthy to be done, the said creature followed full of tears and devotion. With bitter weeping, nay with violent sobbing, she fell into a trance crying *"I die, I die!"* And when she was helped upright by her sisters it was plain for all to see that her palms were bloody. Although she was seen to be suffering great pain as we say in *imitatio Christi*, the beatific vision allowed her to endure the rapture of her miraculous fusion.

Again, after kneeling and praying for many hours she came to herself with her arms spread wide. Then it was that she felt as if her side had been gashed open but she could not open her habit for the wounds on her palms. After a while and with much suffering she succeeded in loosening her habit. A wound the size of a single span had opened at her right side, from which water and blood purled forth. During her ecstasies she was said to have emitted the sweet odour of sanctity, a fragrance associated with high virtue.

Neither is the foregoing exceptional in the experience of the priest who is writing this book. A novice at Ghent who contracted the stigmata bled copiously every Friday from the time of their first appearance to her death at the age of three and thirty. It was said that she lived without food, only taking the Holy Communion and that sparingly, her face was frequently covered with a mask of blood from the circlet of thorns above her head, and her mouth was glutted with blood. Her suffering was extreme and continuous, during which she would oftentimes cry out, *"Aah Lord, because of your great pain, have* mercy. *And if you wish, Lord, send me patience, for otherwise I may not endure my little pain."*

This same novice predicted that after her death her heart would bear images of cross and chalice, the same being truly prophesied, as witnessed by this priest, whereby an examination of the said organ was conducted immediately following her death. Afterwards, her body remained supple, occasionally emitting a scent of freshly opened rosebuds. The stigmata were traceable on her palms and the soles of her feet by a transparency of tissues, and there remained a very considerable curvature of the right shoulder which bent the bone just as the weight of a heavy cross might have done.

Because the Soul expresses the body perfectly and precisely, the wounds of the stigmatic will bear their marks before the throne of God. So says the good priest who was written of before and who was the confessor of Bella-Marie Lambe and her true scribe.

✢ HERE ENDETH THE FIRST BOOK ✢

Gentle Reader,

Some stories are told only to get rid of. It is for this reason, I suspect, that Halpern brought me his armful of facts and folders, his maze of transcripts with their handwritten cogitations, this story wrapped in tissue paper. And I am not like the scribe who murmurs, *may God grant me the wisdom and grace to be the faithful chronicler.* No indeed. I resolved at once that this was the story I would keep for myself, ornamenting and inventing at will. Besides, up until now Halpern has been so inept that someone else must surely take over.

I must not allow myself to be unduly influenced by the irrational. There was a time, in the prefix of my misspent youth, when I was something of a rogue woman, crashing through days, my wiring awry. Farmer Bob, a long-suffering man with slow hands and a drawl like a lasso, often had occasion to remind me of the body's secret excesses: the headaches, the blackouts, the bruises on my arms he said were self-inflicted.

Why do I believe him? I believe him. Because I could offer no
natural explanation, I began to suspect the unnatural. Such
was Halpern's dilemma, such was Ginny's.

But they are children, those two! Halpern dragging his alba-
tross pity, at once fascinated and appalled. Do you think this
is a place abandoned by God? I once asked him. It seems
whenever you ask me a question it's because you already know
the answer, he replied. He threw up his hands in that characteristic gesture of his, triangular and undismayed, as if declining
to overstate what we both already know: that the flesh may
be tempted both according to nature and against nature. The
palms of his hands were ascetic looking, with ruts cloven
between lines of head and heart.

As for Virginie, that girl is not well. She goes about with torn
eyes and a mouth that brings to mind nothing so much as
the verb *gnaw*. I think she suspects that she believed her own
authority too easily. She imagines she is a skeptic, question of
mind over mirror. Last night I dreamed of her. She was lying
naked on a beach, her body a shell, hard and limned at the
edges. Empty, untempted. Drifts of sand blew between the hairs
on her forearm. At once I was both dreamer and dreamed, I
looked down at myself, at the foreshortened view from between
my own breasts, my stomach taut, thighs sprung. This was the

one place from which no-one could see me, from which I could
not be seen. The last time we took tea together in my kitchen,
Ginny and I, she asked me, with touching faith in my reply, if
I thought she'd been remiss in her diagnosis of the Desjardins
girl. Where, she asked, does one go to examine the miraculous?
I patted her cheek but did not answer because if I told her, she
would only begin to search in all the wrong places.

But the miraculous is not a word I would use, either lightly or
otherwise. Besides, these days it is nothing more than an adjec-
tive, all the powder worn off its wings by hasty fingers. I prefer
the word mysterious. There is always a solution to mystery:
words written in lemon juice that appear on the page when
gently warmed over an open flame, a pair of heavy footprints
in the snow. What comforts me about the mystery is how the
solution proves the structure. And then there's the indelible
charm of the labyrinth; the closer you move towards a centre,
the greater the danger. At pains to conceal a secret of the first
magnitude, there are eye-witnesses and rumour-mongers,
someone always chosen to look in the wrong direction! By
idolizing reason we fail to see the obvious.

The miracle's first condition is one of verifiability, three assorted
Vicars of God, and the signature of the Archbishop only just
sufficient as proof. I imagine the accounts that are prepared,

written in some detail but without undue exaggeration and forwarded to his Excellency, the Pope. He says nothing because there is nothing to be said. Silently and in the uneven stutter of candlelight, the miracle is formally witnessed. Does this mean that a miracle is marked by an excess of language, or by its absence? A cupful of honey is passed around afterwards for each man to taste for himself the grace of God, obstinate and tactile. And, like the storyteller, the Creator is present at this ceremony by proxy. *I am who you don't see. I am what is implied.*

On a more mundane note, it has begun to rain again. These days my progress is slow and painful, I feel almost as old as Mina Isaacs. Franklin dodges mutinously about my feet as we go out to the woodshed together. We leave a trail of footprints in my newly-dug vegetable garden. Franklin's are like a row of lightly pursed kisses, but my own are improbably articulate against the loosely sprung soil. Looking back I realize that my footprints have been made by a woman much heavier than I am, one who carries the burden of others upon her shoulders.

Daniel now, clearly he is unwell. His face has the medieval pallor of candle wax, and his body gives the impression of somehow having broken through its own element. He is no longer of the earth but of the air, his flesh consigned to the purifying flames of some attenuated illness which he declines

to name. These last few nights when he came to my house for
a drink before retiring to his motel room, he communicated
only an immense and wordless weariness. Halpern, I said, in
reply to his many anxieties, there's no progress in knowledge.
No indeed, there is only ingenious recapitulation.

Like me, Halpern does not believe in the devil. Like me, he sees
evidence of devilry everywhere. Some would say that without
fear of the devil there is no more need of God. *Afterwards* is, in
any case, a magnificent counterfeit, our broken bodies gathered
unto God. Isn't that how Massimo would put it? Returned to
the good Lord, that last nave and transept of the soul. Even
now, I imagine Him fading slowly from the world, snuffed out
like Tinkerbell by our collective unbelief. *I could not save them
all,* He whispers with His last breath, *so I saved none.* It is at
times like this that I feel a familiar yet entirely secular compas-
sion for God.

Well, whatever is sickening Halpern, few would accuse him of
spiritual unease. He is entirely too pragmatic in his belief that
a town like ours can be taken in stride. All day he walks up
and down Main street, making notes, taking photographs, little
sense to his direction unless you can begin to believe, as he
clearly does, that no detail is irrelevant. Watching him zippered
into his all-weather parka, his extraordinary hands carefully,

tastefully, gloved, none would suspect him of the excesses that
have distended his subterranean life thus far. Love—for want
of a better word—*love*, that amorous melancholy, our saltflesh
surging at odds with the tide, a body that opens and closes
like a harbour-lock, a bridge. Halpern, I told him, after an
evening of white wine and fresh pickerel in which he confided
a profound horror at his suspected tendency, his—and I quote
—*proneness*, well, if not to the flight then at least to the fall;
Halpern, I imagine that like all of us, you love immensely,
imprecisely, and almost entirely to avoid loving. He shuffled his
eyes away from mine, by which I knew his unrequited habit was
still strong. Well, he is not the first to believe that a wounded
heart is larger, more habitable because broken open.

We long for what is missing, the moment that is not yet written.
The mind, unable to recollect itself, embarks on all manner
of well-told lies: long lists of inarticulate ailments, rumour,
confused genealogies, the intricate and deceptive folds of memory. Love can't be sustained on such a high note, there is a
need to turn our attention, even momentarily, to less exalted
things: the passing of fathers, the delusion of mirrors, water
and its delicate flounces as it is poured. Somewhere high above
us, a star tunes its tines on the sky's metallic blue, illustrating
the predicament of the metaphor—always elsewhere.

Gentle reader, ignore the obvious, the storyteller's prevarication!
The past is something that happens at a remove, to others. I
have no memory, I remain perpetually in parentheses between
amnesia and hearsay, trying to recall not only what has
already happened, but what can only be imagined, like stone,
and metamorphoses, and the perfect death. In a disquisition
on lying I would have to take grave exception to the word *like*,
the lying word, the word that tries to splice the metaphysics of
word and thing.

An unbeliever, Halpern still struggles to keep life from turning
to anecdote. His return to a place, for instance, memorized in
early childhood and apparently indelible. Perhaps that's why
he seems unable to proceed with this story, unable to ask questions, or at least not the right ones. The past for him is the
unread, *unrequited* story, the place he can neither imagine
nor recall. As for the child, as for Donna, what can one say?
I knew her when she was little, even before she went to school.
One day, soon after her father left, she came over to me at the
drugstore, ducked her head once before asking me to help her
choose a birthday card for that benighted brother of hers. She
couldn't read yet, you see, but she paid with a spill of coins
wrapped in newspaper. The cashier helped her count the
change, then she carefully twisted the remaining coins into
the paper in a gesture at once tender and acquisitive. Every

time I saw her after that she was standing on one leg or the other, never both.

Only last summer she helped me when the cat pushed out her kittens, the hot wind pulling a kited sky backwards and forwards above our heads. Together we named the four kittens, neat and black as musical notes: Crotchet, Minim, Quaver, and Treble. Five days later Donna brought me the waterlogged smallest, the only one to survive when the remaining string section of the quartet was drowned in the slough. She has a history of these artful discoveries. Poor Donna, her mother tells me, always being the first to find dead animals, the fallen nestlings of spring, the flyblown corpses of little things in tall grass.

Believe me, I've done everything short of asking her what happened the day she began bleeding. But I don't want that tender mind cut open. Besides, she is frighteningly honest, will admit to anything. Donna is the book we are all trying to read. Ginny, in her log cabin flooded with light from windows set in the angles of walls. Halpern, the journalist, who has undertaken to write notes as another way to evade love, avoid death. And myself, alone with my large-print edition of Proust, watching the hot summer rain sizzling against the window panes. I am tempted to place a call to a late-night radio station, request a song about love, something to raid the appetite, bring the nerves to the surface of the skin. If only to remind myself of the body I once had.

Some stories are told to get rid of. Some stories you keep for yourself. I propose to continue this journey begun by others, because I have finally learned that truth is proven by the resistance it overcomes. Take Halpern, for instance, he speaks of silence with eloquence, lists the things he has declined to name. Meanwhile, before our very eyes, his body blisters and burns, silently claiming guilt for the crime he has not yet committed. Observe the blood blisters on the underside of his tongue, the weeping cold sores at the corner of his mouth.

Why do I talk, with such passion and resentment, of the past? The only progress possible is through storytellers who know that history is always present. Poor Halpern, with his visible seams, his conditional replies. Sometimes, when he stretches out before me in a chair by the fire, I swear I can see the graveworms crawling in his folds as he tries to warm his hands against the coffee mug. He is already burnt flesh.

We talked of what the newspapers called the Annex Blood Miracles. With what I can only describe as a kind of medieval fervour, he embarked upon a history of the transformations of the body. Well, a classical education is sure to distinguish one in later life. Halpern, I wanted to say, what you are suffering from is the absence of transcendence in your life. Instead, I decided to make a new pot of coffee, I offered him one of papa's *Schimmel-pennincks,* and directed the conversation away from this horrified contemplation of genesis.

Poor man, he fell asleep soon after, his hair dark and restless against his damp forehead. I watched him in the murmur of candlelight: heavy flanked from the waist down, with clumpy thighs to pitch a cleanrun boy's chest. His eyes fluttered a little, for he was dreaming of what evaded him, even through the mesh of lists he had thrown. On his face as he slept was long-ing, a half-smile undiminished by expectation. Yes, I might have been a lover gazing at the clandestine body of her beloved! Momentarily overtaken, I wanted him and I wanted him to want me. And I wanted nothing. And— Imagine, at my age! But it was a figment of the moment—luckily, the sense I have developed most strenuously is my sense of direction—an enchantment maliciously visited upon me by some displaced ill-wish. Or had you not heard that the devil is pitch-forking about these parts?

The second time he came to Annex, Halpern stayed with me, because by then the place was overrun by reporters determined to read into the blood miracles a geography of myth and fear. The town was convulsed with matters of belief. Not everyone believed, there were still those who cried *trickery* or *treachery* or even *madness*. Geisler, for instance, never deviated from the firmly held conviction that we were all making bitter fools of ourselves. He declined to offer any opinion on events save to suggest, by example, that those with work to do had better ways to occupy their time. But for the most part, those who didn't believe in the mystery of the stigmata had no trouble in proposing equally mysterious phenomena of their own. Many who were skeptical at the thought of religious intervention, for instance, found it easy to imagine an alien presence in our midst. There was a renewed interest in witchcraft, poltergeists, and extra-terrestrial abductions, as if these explanations, being contemporary, were more acceptable than mystical possession.

Not surprisingly, most of the religious leaders in town evidenced caution in their judgements, advising their assorted flocks to believe with their hearts and not their eyes. Massimo Ricci particularly seemed unwilling to indulge in speculation about the "miracle" that had taken place, seemed barely able to hide his resentment of the crowds that gathered each dusk on the church lawns. This attitude surprised me at first. Like many others, I had often been witness to his adoration of the sainted Padre Pio, and I could not now understand his reluctance to welcome the miraculous into his life. I soon realized, however, that for Massimo life was not continuous with art and that his passion for the Padre fell into the latter category as an experience to be studied, written about, adored from a distance, but not to be emulated. I don't mean to imply that he was a bad Catholic, or that he didn't believe the incarnation was possible in his Parish, only that such had not yet been demonstrated in his presence or to his satisfaction. And he was agitated by the *messiness*, he did not appreciate blood on his altar or litter in his grotto. Like a fastidious Lady Macbeth, he went about with upraised hands. *What, in my house!* his pursed lips and raised brows seemed to imply.

The other person who was deeply and unhappily affected by the crisis that summer was Virginie. She alternately suspected that she had believed too easily or not enough, and her scrupulous conscience gave her no respite. Of course I refer here to her diagnosis of Donna Desjardins as a psychosomatic and not to her belief or disbelief in the child's saintliness. She was disturbed by the piety that racked our town that year, and by the equally profound need on the part of most people to make their devotions public. A firmly committed disciple of causality, Ginny would have liked nothing better than to sieve the child's mind to the chaff that she knew could explain whatever it was she most despaired of knowing. But she was so appalled by

the child's suffering, and so relieved the bleeding had stopped,
that nothing could have persuaded her to intervene. Still, she
suffered. Like all empiricists she suffered from the absence of
evidence, the suspicion that evidence would convince nobody,
least of all herself.

I know she was reading a book Massimo Ricci had lent her
about the life of a Saint, and such an uncharacteristic conces-
sion on her part worried me. I left small gifts of fruitcake
and crabapple jelly at her door and tried to entice her to my
kitchen to resume our late night chats, but I suspect she disap-
proved of Halpern and as long as he was my guest she made
her excuses and stayed away. As for the rest of us, that summer
was brimming with scandal and speculation. Everywhere we
went in those days—to Foodtown, the hospital, to church—
we were confronted by cameras, microphones, pens poised to
take down our words. I was obliged to take refuge in irony, an
expedient that few, besides Halpern, appreciated. Truthful only
about my propensity for lying, I posed arguments as solutions,
indulged in an improvisatory flow of hearsay and supposition.

All this time Halpern played the journalist, his concerns
remained limited, accurate, local. He would admit to no
thoughts of his own, and try as I might I could not force him
to share his research, let alone his opinions. I suspected him

of deliberately withholding his friendship at this time, holding within him only the form of his own perfect emptiness. He, more than anyone else, resented the intrusion of faith in his undiluted life and he grew increasingly pale, weary. One night towards the end, I opened his notebook and read what he had written before falling asleep in the armchair. Listen:

> At few other times have there been so many
> moments in which confession and secrecy
> intersect. Nevertheless, something still
> eludes us. In being translated into words,
> the body, in the end, eludes us.

The Blood Girl

"My brother's name is Adam, when I was born my father wanted me to be the first of something too, so they called me Dawn, then Donna. But everyone calls me Donna now."

The young girl who opened the door to Halpern and was now sitting sidesaddle on the arm of her grandmother's chair had evidently just had a bath because her hair was damp and knuckled. Her skin had a solvent quality as if in danger of dissolving a little at the edges.

"Hush now," her grandmother quieted her with a sickle hand across her knees, "your mum'll be home soon and you know she don't like you talking to the news. Would you like a cup of coffee, mister?"

She leaned into the doorway, half turned toward the garishly lit kitchen, evidently afraid to leave Donna alone with Halpern. At that moment, the screen door grated metal and a woman entered, her knuckles white with the weight of a string shopping basket jammed with letters. Donna was sent upstairs to bathe the baby, and the grandmother, whose name was never offered, passed gratefully through the doorway and into her kitchen, from which the oddly disturbing smell of ripe bacon and greens proceeded.

Transcript of Interview between Mrs. Kennedy Desjardins and
Daniel Halpern: Desjardins' House, May 5th: 4:30 p.m.

KD. That thing on? Okay, look I can't give you much time, this business has already taken months out of my life. Do you see that bag?
Full of letters. We've been getting so many letters, Sheila at the post-office had to get us another box.

DH. *Who are the letters from?*

KD. Folks. Everyone who's ever seen Jesus in a tortilla shell. Cranks, exorcists, people bearing witness, sharing the light. This woman wrote last week, she was fixing her husband's breakfast down in Tulsa when her hands began to itch and burn. She went into a kind of trance and when she came to her hands were hot and sticky with something, and blood had begun to pool around the fried eggs in her pan. Every Easter she gets the wounds. Says she can lose up to a pint of blood on Good Friday. But she's not the kind wants to be in the spotlight. Says she wore gloves in public for five years. Now she wants to have a hysterectomy, her doctor says it might help. Wants to know what I think!

DH. *Did it happen as suddenly with Donna?*

KD. Yes, sudden.

DH. *What happened exactly?*

KD. They called me up from the school, said your kid is bleeding but we can't see anything wrong. Thought at first she'd got her period. Well I rushed over and brought her to the hospital, they don't know nothing about medicine over at that school. Dr. Ginny, she saw my Donna, looked all over the palm of her hand with a magnifying glass, very carefully. I said, what are you looking for? She said, for whatever

caused the blood Mrs. Desjardins, but don't worry, it doesn't look like
there's anything there. And she bandaged Donna's hand and gave her
a hug, said she could go back to school. Three hours later she was
back in hospital, right hand this time. Dr. Ginny booked her directly
into the wards, said she'd have to stay overnight, ran tests, drew
blood *ha ha*. Even put her on one of those heart machines the hospital's just bought. By then grandma and I knew what was going
on and we wanted Father Ricci. They had to let us take her home
because there was nothing wrong. All their tests came back negative
and it looked like she'd stopped bleeding. When we got home I sat
her on the kitchen table and started to undress her. Her right sock
was already soaked through. Look over there, you can just see the
blood in the heel of that footprint over there, we still can't get it out
of the carpet.

There was always something special about my Donna. When
she was born the doctors had to knock me out, something to do
with the placenta. While I slept they lifted her from my pouch, *pick-
pockets* I called them when I woke up. And then she's always been so
good to that brother of hers. From a young age she helped me look
after him, tying his shoes in the morning, seeing his fly was done up.
And when that friend of hers, Marie-Clare, drowned, she was heart-
broken. They say kids don't mourn for long but it was a good twelve
months before she got over it. That child has no skin at all when it
comes to grief.

Way I knew her grieving was over was she let her hair grow out.
See when we first heard of the accident up at Leaf Rapids, my Donna
she took a scissors and cut off her hair. Just like that, not a word. This
white-faced kid had bitten her lip through to stop from crying and

when I got to her she was standing in front of the mirror with her hair in swatches around her, sticking up from the carpet.

But you did that too, mamma, she said, when I asked her what the hell she thought she was doing, cut off your hair when daddy left. Aah Donna, I wanted to tell her, do what I say, not what I do.

Funny thing is, she used to comb her hair as if it was one of those phantom limbs, nothing there but you still feel the itch. Every night before bed I'd hear her brushing the air round her shoulders, talking to little Marie-Clare. Just normal things that children say, like what they ate for supper and what they did at school. Father Ricci said not to pay attention, said it'd wear off over time. It did but now this happens, and the poor child's at the centre of things again. Still got to see Dr. Ginny every two weeks for check-ups and like that, although if you ask me, that woman's getting a little above herself.

DH. *What about Donna's dad?*

KD. Her dad's dead. Even before he died he had no expectations, though. His mum went down with drink and a trucker on the Number 6 pull to Thompson. He lost his first wife to the northern line too, Donna's dad. Kind of man was always buying shoes of cow-hide leather whatever else he couldn't afford. When I met him he was living in Lavallee with a girl just out of school, virgins once removed we used to call them. Not that he would've approved.

DH. *Do you approve?*

KD. Well, that's not the way I'd put it really. I mean, as Father Ricci says, the Holy Ghost has a mind of His own. But, it's just not my way, Mr. Halpern, not Donna's way either, if the truth be told. Down at the hospital we have spray guns and hoses, anti-septic cleaners and long rubber gloves. The A-team, that's what we call ourselves. No cleaning emergency too big to handle. That's how I think of sin too, something that leaves lime scales and rust stains on the body. Something that can be wiped over, scrubbed away. And why *my* little girl, why my Donna, is what I want to know. Why not Mother Teresa or Father Ricci's old mum or—

There was a sharp cry from the kitchen and the sound of something metal hitting the floor. Before Halpern could react, Kennedy Desjardins had flung herself through the door and into the kitchen. When Halpern entered he saw her bent over her mother who was holding one hand patiently over the sink. Although blood was flowing from between her fingers she was careful to keep it from spattering into the fresh greens she had been slicing. At the same moment a baby in an upstairs room began to wail thinly, and an older boy whom Halpern had not at first seen huddled himself closer into a dark corner.

At first Halpern imagined, with wild dismay, that another blood miracle was in the process of occurring, but then he saw the curved scraping knife, the chopping block.

"Look, mum's lopped the top off her thumb, it's those damn turnips, don't know why they have to grow them so hard. I can't leave the baby, can you take her to the hospital?"

Halpern helped the older woman, who had started to tremble with shock, into her coat. He only looked back once. Kennedy Desjardins was on her knees on the floor in front of the boy whose eyes were tightly closed and who was rhythmically banging his head against the door frame.

Halpern

S u d d e n l y it started to snow again. Halpern was anxious to get back to Winnipeg. He had information to gather, promises to keep, and a story to beat onto the page. His impatience was saline, like the taste in his mouth these last three mornings, waking on the edge of the long highway out of town as if he were an obscure character in a story that had moved on years ago, when the train still came through town every day and twice on Wednesdays.

In truth, it was his fastidious dismay in the face of nature's plotless direction that goaded him to pack his bags. But he reckoned without it being Saturday when the gas station on the edge of town opened an hour later than usual, accommodating its proprietor's Friday night hangover. So Halpern found himself sitting again at the corner table of Jeane's Bake Shop. A kind of low-grade sadness lapped at the edges of the morning. Outside, snow fell insistently, without beginning or end. ∎

Worknotes

Father Massimo Ricci

- A voluptuary uneasy with mysticism, he tries to convince himself of the body's incorruptibility but is dedicated to sensual, mortal things; thick carpets, thick butter.

- The kind of Catholic priest who likes smells and bells, liturgical music and incense, takes a naive delight in such accompaniments.

- One recognizes a cloying self-doubt at the base of him, overlain by God. It is God who allows him to speak in a powerful voice, assume disguises, give counsel. Either that or Padre Pio.

- These things make him evasive on the subject of Donna's stigmata. After all, he, more than anyone, is required to believe in the religious implications of her wounds. Yet he seems wary, concerned to protect the child from scrutiny.

- Surprised by his candour. Realize Father Ricci has seldom been interviewed, never quoted. Perhaps he was cautioned by his Archbishop or whatever, when the Press first descended. Now that it's over he can relax, give in to his impulses.

Donna Desjardins

- Strange evocative name, *Madonna of the Gardens*.

- Strangely evocative child, but curiously blank. I've the feeling she's a notebook for other people to write upon. No, that's too fanciful, and yet, Virginie Waters, Father Ricci, her mother, they all have so much to say about her.

- Her mother is the kind of woman who says, "never leave before the teacup is cold." Donna is a well-behaved child and by all accounts a devoted sister.

Halpern

A n   o l d   man shuffled over to Halpern's table. "You the news?" he asked, moving his mouth carefully around the three short words. One of his arms was missing but he moved in rapid staccato so that his denim shirt sleeve assumed a life of its own, grotesquely caressing the table.

"It's the black birds bring the snow," he said pointing outside where two or three disreputable crows shuffled crook-legged on the side of the road. "It's what they hide beneath their wings, flying north for the summer. We call it crazysnow. Comes after the last snow, when you know for sure it's done for good. Crows'll get you every time, making April fools of honest folks. You the news?"

When Halpern nodded, he hunted rapidly through his pockets, pulling out papers and springs, oily bits and pieces of metal and wood. "Can't find it. Anyhow, I'm to give you a message. I'm to tell you that little Donna Desjardins, she's not the only blood girl in this town. There's someone else got the marks but she's not making a show of it.

Not yet at any rate. That's all."

"Who told you to give me the message?" Halpern took hold of the empty shirtsleeve to keep the other at his side, but the old man snatched it back and regarded him for a moment, his head on one side, his eyes bright with malice or, for all Halpern knew, humour.

"Used to be a trapper up North when I was disarmed by a grizzly. Now I know enough to keep my eyes open and my mouth shut. Good day to you." The crows flew up at his approach and for a moment the air outside was printed with dark scimitar wings. The waitress who came up to deliver Halpern's eggs clucked derisively.

"Wasn't a grizzly that got him but the snow he slept in, so drunk he was feeling no pain till they took off his arm at the clinic." ∎

Halpern's Second List of Oddities and Strange Occurrences

1) Unless you live near a railway line you won't see trains pass your window. Perhaps Ricci meant that we have to be open to mysteries for them to happen, and to witness them we have to be in the right time at the right place. Here in Annex, for instance, in the last five years of the twentieth century. Apocalyptics would say the world is speeding up, spinning off its axis.

2) But why, as Mrs. Desjardins said, should it happen to Donna? The mystery is completely arbitrary and entirely precise, a force in itself, one that picks out its own victim, its own heroine. Aside from the fact, of course, that the subject has to be a certain kind of person. A psychosomatic, as Virginie would say—no hyphen between the body and the mind.

3) Here's the thing. An old guy comes up to this journalist, says, I've got something to tell you, says, someone sent me but I won't say who. Says, something's going to happen but I won't say what. This is not a mystery until it's fulfilled, only a mystery in retrospect.

4) All mysteries occur in retrospect. The way people remember Donna backwards. Delma telling me how she used to walk with her brother every evening to the post-office. Ricci's story about the friend who drowned. There is a before to the mystery as significant as the mystery.

5) While we're on the subject, there's never a mystery until the frame-up. Someone who comes in from outside, says look, there is method in this madness, tell me your story. The mystery is about stories moving reluctantly into light. An existing pattern occurs slightly out of sequence. We are

required to put the pattern back together again. Our position vis à vis the mystery is a priori, we come in after the fact. We leave via the solution.

6) Like readers we rely strictly on chronology, therefore we are ourselves part of the sequence. The mystery doesn't end with the solution but continues.

7) This is, of course, the argument of a Jesuit, an expert in mysteries.

1st Parish of the Interlake
Desk of Father Massimo Ricci
7 May 1995 Year of Our Lord

Archdiocese
City of Winnipeg

Your Excellency,

I want to thank you, profoundly, for the comfort you have offered me during this time. Without your guidance I would have felt unworthy to proceed in this matter, since my knowledge of the miraculous extends only as far as my admiration for Padre Pio, the noted saint and protector of Foggia in Italy.

Of course I have kept your admonition always foremost in mind. That the church must proceed with extreme caution in matters of this kind, that the child must at all costs be protected, and that the Press must not be allowed to make of this possibly miraculous occurrence what is popularly called a *circus*.

I am pleased to report that the child is in good health and in the protective custody of her mother. Since the bleeding has, as you know, apparently ended, the hospital has no further jurisdiction in this matter. Despite her profound and no doubt frightening

experience, the young girl remains a stable, healthy child. Her
mother tells me that she is regaining her confidence and has begun
to attend school again. As you advised, I have kept a careful watch
over the family and pride myself that no spiritual harm may come
to them, for they are constantly in my prayers. In addition, I have
seen Donna Desjardins privately and ascertained to my satisfaction
that she remains a good Catholic girl, attending confession regularly and preparing for her communion.

With regard to publicity, I am pleased to assure you that the
Press has been adequately subdued. Of course I have not entirely
been able to control the interviews that the mother, Kennedy
Desjardins, has seen fit to give. And despite my strongest recom-
mendations, she has, at times, been overly emphatic in her
narration of events. Nevertheless, I have insisted, and I might add
succeeded, in impressing upon her that the child not be allowed to
give interviews.

I myself have at times been the recipient of requests by the
Press to comment on the matter. I have refused all but the most
courteous of these and have remained a devoted and respectful
servant of the Church's Will. I might be permitted to give you a
short example of this sentiment: yesterday I was approached by a
most refined yet humble journalist. I permitted him a short interview, where we discussed miracles and the ineffability of Divine
Will. I give you my assurance that what I flatter myself to call
such *diplomacy* will continue to be my strategy in this business.

My dear Father, I will end now with my respects and profound gratitude once again. Mother says you will not take it amiss for her to send her love, she is an old woman and may be permitted such effusions! I trust that you will inform me of the Vatican's intercession in this matter.

May the Lord bless and keep you.

Yours in Christ,
[Father] Massimo Ricci.

Virginie Waters
Box 350
Annex

6 May '95

Darling Lashia

How goes life in Montréal? I miss it all so much although I don't regret leaving as you know. Indeed I'm grateful to be away from the old grief, at least geographically, and here seemed as good a place as any to alight.

My little log cabin is cozy as ever and Molly, my landlady, continues to be a delight. From where I sit at my window writing to you, I can see her walking across the lawn to inspect her fences, her terrier following one step behind. There, she has turned and waved to me. Imagine, a woman of some seventy years in such health and good spirits!

I come a little sheepishly to the point. My last letter was frantic, I know and I apologize. My dear, I didn't mean to make you anxious, truly it was overwork, exhaustion and the strain of the moment. That business I told you, with the little Catholic girl, really upset me. You'll be pleased to hear the bleeding has stopped, the Press have departed and the town returned to normal.

When I think back on it, I can't help feeling that I've been remiss. I've been over and over it all in my mind. And you're quite right when you say it isn't the undiagnosed that frightens me anymore but the unknown. We both know what a skeptic I am, why, I don't even believe in summer anymore!

That's just a crack about the weather, we get used to making them in Annex. A couple of days ago the spring thaw began and the streets were flooded with rivulets and streams. The ditches at the sides of the road rose to hip height and most of the children are down in them at this very minute looking for mud-suckers, beset, no doubt, with all manner of bacterial infections in the process.

I'll end now as I'm exhausted but just wanted to write a short note to reassure you. Your friend is not going stir-crazy, the warm weather is almost here and please god this whole bloody business will soon be behind us. I send you all my love and an open invitation to come and visit me soon,

XXX
Ginny.

Mrs. Grace Mae Peel
Gary, Indiana
1/5/95

Dear Donna

I read your story in the newspapers down here, they are
making quite a fuss about it, I can tell you. The Reverend Harry
Tomlinson of the First Baptist Revival Church of Indiana says that
you sound like a blessed child and so I'd like to share an experience
of my own. We are all children of the Lord together, one day in
Heaven we shall know each other by a glance of the soul, as the
blessed Saint Elizabeth Ann Seton would say, who you may know
was the first American saint.

Well, I was cleaning my house one day, washing the floors
and vacuuming the carpets. There's something about cleaning that
is very restful for me. As I scrub away at the windows, then wipe
them down with a dry chamois cloth, I imagine the scum that has
collected all week on my soul is also being washed away. Holiness
does not lie in doing great things. As Mother Teresa of Calcutta
has said, it lies in doing little things with great love. Love is the
one true alchemy in this world, transforming the base metals of
hardship into the gold of redemption.

Just as I was finishing the last indoor window—I live in a
two storey walk-up so there are a lot of windows—I saw the face

of our Lord in the spray of detergent as it fell and spread out against the glass.

Donna, you have known in yourself the moment of redemption so there is no need to describe the terror and the love I knew. My eyes were filled with piercing light, my body became crystal and shattered in the sun, in my ears was the sound of angelic voices. I remained in a trance before the window for the remainder of the day and was found prostrated before it by my husband. As soon as I awoke I turned my hungry eyes to the glass but, soapsuds being what they are, the beloved face had melted into the air.

My dear, take courage from this story. You are not alone in your salvation. Remember, "by perseverance even the snail reaches the Ark." May God bless you my child, you are always in my prayers.

In Christ's Love,
(Mrs.) Grace Mae Peel.

Halpern

At the Art Gallery in Winnipeg, Halpern waited for some time, walking idly about an exhibit of Chinese Porcelain and listening to the tick of winter run-off against the eaves. The woman who finally walked toward him was taut and angular, seeming to flash sullenly in the dim museum light. When she got closer he realized that the slightly venomous glow she exuded came from a series of subtly arranged points about her body; the silver buckles of shoes and belt, her bright teeth. Her hair was cropped and mobile and swung aside to reveal some kind of quartz arrangement at the lobes of her elegant ears.

She drew him behind her in a phosphorescent wake until the two were seated in her underground office where she listened with an absorption that seemed to penetrate the walls. The space between them quickly grew porous, avid. When she spoke, he noticed flakes of flint set like mica in her colour-less eyes.

"What you are telling me isn't new. So you've come to the realization that the body has a history?" ∎

Transcript of Interview between Dr. Helena Skuros and Daniel
Halpern: Winnipeg Art Gallery, May 8th: 4 p.m.

HS. You want to know about blood miracles? Well, quite simply, in
the late Middle Ages blood began to appear on hands and faces, on
walls and wafers. This was the beginning of what we have come to
call the blood miracles. They took place primarily on the bodies of
women and took two forms. You already know about stigmata, the
other is the miracle of the bleeding host, where consecrated Eucharist
wafers turn into bleeding flesh. Like stigmata, this is a miracle of the
female genre.

DH. *What's the significance of the high proportion, what is it—
seven to one—of female mystics? Something to do with misogyny,
repression?*

HS. I've no interest in discussing this in terms of power structures or
abnormal psychology. You're quite correct, all but two documented
cases of visible stigmata are female. But let me at least caution you
against projecting a twentieth-century sensibility on the medieval
aesthetic. If *we* eroticize the body and define ourselves by the nature
of our sexuality, can we assume the same of another time? No,
emphatically not. All evidence shows that medieval images of the
body have less to do with sexuality than with fertility, decay. Don't
forget that female spirituality at that time was incarnational, even
bizarrely somatic.

DH. *A psychosomatic symbiosis between body and mind?*

HS. Or body and soul. Let me give you an example. When Hadewijch,
the Flemish poet, described herself embracing Christ, feeling Him
penetrate her, losing herself in an ecstasy from which she reluctantly

returned, she described this experience as the love of God. When
the medieval nuns Lukardis of Oberweimar and Margaret of Faenza
breathed deeply into their sisters' mouths and felt "sweet delight
flooding their members," they too described this experience as one
of love. The list continues; Rupert of Deutz, a twelfth century monk,
climbs on the altar, embraces the crucifix and feels Christ's tongue
in his mouth. Catherine of Siena receives Christ's foreskin as a wedding ring by which she promises to appropriate His pain. It is we, you
and I, who suspect sexual intentions in these medieval virgins and
ascetics for whom sexuality was the least of the world's temptations.

DH. *But it seems evident from what you say that bodily . . . agitation
accompanied love of God in the Middle Ages.*

HS. Yes, yes, but what worried medieval thinkers was not whether
the sensations were sexual or chaste, but whether they were inspired
by God or sent by the devil. There was no division between the physical and the spiritual, between this world and the next. The evidence
of the shared suffering with Christ, however acquired, would have
been enough to inspire awe. As for twentieth century readers, who
can blame them for being literal, secular, with a tendency to find sexuality more compelling than decay, suffering, or salvation!

DH. *Yes, but—*

HS. In fact we're dealing here not with a sickness of the body but a
failure of language. Something lost to translation. The movement from
mystic to hysteric is not only the movement from medieval to modern.

DH. *But why? I mean why the appearance of the stigmata at all?*

HS. Like everything else they appear and reappear in periods of eco-
nomic depression. When the material world disappoints, the faithful
seek signs and reassurances. As late as this century, after the second

world war, three hundred statues moved in churches all over Italy. As for the thirteenth century, the stigmata appeared in a period where many factors converged. There was a reaction against the corrupt and worldly church of the day. At the same time God was presented as a human being, a physical body who suffered the pains of the flesh on the cross. Mysticism was a way for lay people, particularly women, to gain access to the body of Christ. Through prayer, meditation, austerity, even self-inflicted pain, these holy women were able to commune with Christ *as body*. In my opinion, stigmata were viewed by pious women as their reward for mystical devotion, an intense empathy with Christ's suffering body. As for the women, the chosen, they dispensed spiritual advice and wisdom, writing of their mystical experiences, composing prayers, translating and interpreting Scripture. Well, good for them!

DH. *I read that since photographic techniques revealed Christ's wounds as they were positioned in the Turin shroud—as nail marks in the wrists not through the palms—wounds have begun replicating this position in modern stigmatics. Can the form in which wounds appear be traced to religious images?*

HS. Exactly so. In the thirteenth century, representations of Christ's suffering become much more graphic. Blood pours from his wounds, his agonized hands twist towards heaven, while the use of one nail to hold both feet produces a writhing motion that heightens the trajectory of suffering. Perhaps a tradition in which Christ's suffering is graphically portrayed needs to be in place before stigmatics can produce their wounds.

DH. *What about the Church, why were they wary of accepting the testimony of mystic women?*

HS. Naturally, the Church views claims of the miraculous and the supernatural with extreme caution because it doesn't want to yield its authority to "hysterics." Even today! But then it was worse. Do you know that in the thirteenth century, the chapter of the Abbey of Citeaux in France forbade communion to those women who couldn't retain their senses during Mass? Incredible!

DH. *You're telling me that female stigmatics saw themselves as imitating Christ? How is this possible when Christ was, after all, a man?*

HS. Aah, there's the question. You know Daniel, when you first walked in I didn't think you were a man of faith. Well, you'll be surprised to hear there's evidence for the argument that medieval worshippers sometimes saw the body of Christ as female. Was He, after all, not the body of the Church? Did He not die for our sins as only a mother would? And finally, in dying, did He not resurrect —in other words, give birth to—a saved people? Still, how's this relevant to your inquiry? For one thing, what we would now call a fluidly gendered body is celebrated as fertile. I speak of the body on the cross, a body charged with significance, a body suffering and in pain, but also salvic, redemptive. You can imagine that the efforts of the mystic—the bleeding, the pain—are attempts to fuse with Christ at the moment of His humanity, the moment of His death. As for the stigmatic, it's not always possible to tell whether the wounds are inner or outer.

Halpern

Outside the gallery the streets were slick with run off, and the faces of the pedestrians he passed were tender in the attenuated light of early evening. Even a week ago this narrow half-hour would have been lost in darkness. Halpern was tired, his body dragging the familiar malaise, the old pain, but the story, Donna's story was bending his bones with its weight.

He stopped for a moment at a neighbourhood coffee bar, anticipating the bitter patois of Kenyan blend. The woman behind the counter amiably warmed his mug at the hot water spigot before offering it to him, filled to the brim with coffee and—it seemed to him at this burnished moment—love. He wanted to run his fingers over the rim of her cheek bone, to touch the ridge of one curly pink ear. Instead, he contented himself with palming a loony into her bowl of tips. ∎

Halpern's List of Miracles

1) Trances, levitations, catatonic seizures, other forms of bodily rigidity.

2) Miraculous elongation or enlargement of parts of the body.

3) Mystical lactations, miraculous pregnancies.

4) Swellings of sweet mucus in the throat (*globus hystericus*), ecstatic nosebleeds.

5) Inability to subsist upon anything except the Eucharist.

6) Miraculous bodily closures, as in women who neither menstruate nor excrete.

7) Holy Exuding; the scent of roses during bleeding, sweet-smelling oil after death.

8) Pictures etched on hearts, or precious jewels set within the heart and discovered during preparation for burial.

Halpern

I t w a s dark already, and the tenderness that seemed to suffuse the world was tarnished about the edges. Halpern walked through streets now cold and dreary with the absence of faces. He was remembering Molly Rhutabaga, her irritation with his search for origins, words that changed the shape of the mouth if not the world. Night opened red fruit in the eyes of beggars, and Halpern headed for his apartment, sat before his console, scrawled a hasty outline on a notepad, began. A moment later the voice of his editor over the phone interrupted, resinous with excitement.

"You're done already? Well you have to go back to Annex, something's happened. Another bleeder. Some woman called Arnott. Look, how soon can you get back, place is going to be swarming with reporters? Yes, during church services. All over the altar. I don't know. If I knew that I wouldn't have to send you. First thing, hear?"

The weight of the telephone in his hand recalled him to himself. Gently, Halpern replaced the receiver, switched off his computer, stared out the window at the light draining from the edges of the city. Here I am, he thought, here. ▮

End of Part One

Gentle Reader,

It falls to me now, gentle reader, to try to
describe to you the pass to which our town was brought over
the blood miracles that began first on the forehead and palms
of little Donna Desjardins, and which ended many weeks
later, without cure or reprieve. Every redemption brings its
own loss, for months after the last statue had ceased moving
in the grottos of Our Lady of Perpetual Mercy and All Saints
Church, groups of children took to standing vacantly in lonely
fields, their arms flung outward like the little scarecrows they
had become. Our children, once fat as butter, grew thin
and austere with vigilance, grieving the sunflowers with their
decorum. And of course it was not only the children who were
affected. Some absolute law of the permitted and the forbid-
den seemed to give way in our town, leaving us with no
propriety of tense or tone, no surcease. As for Regina Arnott,
well it is often the youngest child who is set apart, who
is—shall we say—*intended* in the grammar of chronology.

Who loves according to her bond, no more no less.

Every few years there's one goes rogue, turns mimic. She was
not believed, that was the condition and premise of her disease.
For Regina, identity was an improvisatory riff, even when we
were young together, Mina Isaacs, Regina and myself. She was
full of inherited silences, misplaced longings, and a dissonant
sense of honour that had her scraping roadkill off the highway.
Now she moves about this house, my home, intently, her hair
hissing as it seethes about her shoulders. There are black marks
in the hollows of her cheeks as if the devil himself has smudged
her eyes with an obscene fingerprint. Stern as pincers she keeps
house for me, staring down dust motes and lime stains, sag-
ging sofa springs and the inevitable lassitude of framed prints.
Franklin and I are cowed by her, we know—he without words,
me in spite of them—that we have failed to measure up to her
austere regard. Aah well, it's too late to rebuke her. For her, love
is the final disfigurement of meaning. A little blood signifies
nothing in the final reckoning.

This house, my home. Do you know that I have never once, *not
once*, considered leaving for even the amount of time it would
take to return. No, I would not leave this place, this town, had
I rubies the colour of flame to warm my old age. It's true I spent
time up North, writing my book and searching for a landscape

unscrutinized by previous inquiry. I was younger then, if not precisely young, and so *vainglorious*—to use one of papa's favourite words—as to believe with a vigour unimpeded by irony, in origin, beginnings, the whole alphabetical enterprise. When I was living up North I had a recurring dream, the details of which elude me, but that always ended in the discovery of a signpost on the great Yukon overpass that spelled out the word *before* in solemn neon.

Aah youth, foolishness. My difficulties with beginnings are no different from Virginie's difficulties with endings. When she came to Annex to undertake what she and I have privately called the Project of her Father by taking over his practice, she hoped to finish the book she had, for so long, avoided reading, the father whose pages must be slit open, her indecipherable, untranslated papa. My late lamented. But the book that does not lie also lies. His eyes were mineral blue at the centre of a flame, and his silence held the promise of wealth amassed behind closed doors. Her life here has been a constant search: the way she devours books, cracks open walnuts, looks impatiently into the throats, the vaginas, the ears of her patients. Ginny, my dear, my daughter, I want to say at these times, what do you think you have lost? Instead, I pour another cup of my excellent China tea, pat her thin wrists fondly, tell her of the time her father and I exchanged our reading glasses, an act of symbiotic unity unparalleled, in my experience, by the contiguity of lips or genitals.

Some days I watch her from this window, walking home from the hospital, the warm flare of her hair crackling in the wind. And I know, I know there are phrases to live by, stories to tell, truths to unearth not proven by the resistances they overcome. *Pauca fecit plura scripsit; foemina tamen magna fuit*—this is what I choose to be known by, an epitaph composed of equal parts *hubris* and humility. *She did little, she wrote more; still she was a great woman.*

There is one more thing about Virginie that has nothing to do with the annotations by which I have chosen to invent her. That she is good, *intensely good,* an unfashionable quality not in the least impeded by its unlikeliness. Aristotle would have bestowed upon her the epithet *virtue.* Her price in that most profligate of times would have been far above rubies. I've seen infants stop crying when she took them from their mother's arms, frightened children in the emergency ward calmed instantly by the grace of her cool palms. When she comes to visit, Franklin cringes as close to her as he can get, he rests his wilful nose on her thigh and she feeds him tidbits while I pretend not to notice. The petunias she planted in late spring are now an improbable white poultice on the earth, they breathe and blow in the slightest wind and introduce, by their profligacy, the corrective of laughter. She has a low voice, that excellent thing in a woman, and hands so gentle they don't even crack the spine of her book as she reads.

Perhaps we, in this modern world, are immune to the experience of virtue. For us virtue is a wound. I inherited not only my father's silences but his stories as well. As for writing, what else allows you to win and lose, to save and spend the coin of your good name? Perhaps I am smaller than the stories I write and continue to write, since for me, the end of writing is the end, not only of my own story, but of my precarious (yes, I'll admit it) existence. But to return to my sweet Virginie—her problem with endings, her difficulties with the miraculous, the undiagnosable, her tentative appetite for love—she does not yet know that you cannot tell a story that is true. You can only tell true stories. Oh, she will try to tell you there are no truthful stories, that she was refused speech, and has retaliated by refusing to speak. As for me, I have avoided mortality, my own death included. I have no need for resurrection.

Virginie Waters' Journal

Monday, 8 May.

There is no doubt, I suppose, that her wounds were self-inflicted. As soon as the blood stopped and I was able to examine the area, I made out the sideways slash of a blade on the underside of each wrist. The shock and the terror, however, were quite real, Regina was unable to speak to me and we had to sedate her before I could begin suturing the wounds. I had the strangest feeling while doing so that thick satin rather than flesh had been slashed open to reveal the gored red twill beneath.

Father Ricci seemed relieved when I told him. I don't blame him, who'd want another blood miracle on their hands? He looked distracted, however, and told me that her cries had attracted attention in the basement where fifty or so diehards were playing bingo, and all had crowded upstairs to bear witness. He hurried off muttering something about setting the matter straight once and for all, an incongruous figure, pear-shaped and gravid in a landscape of careless, insubstantial verticals: trees knocked sideways, wooden fence-poles thumbtacked upright.

I wonder what Father Thomas Honeycombe (Surgeon) would have had to say. Something sanguine no doubt, to go with the matter at hand. He was nothing if not inventive in his anatomical discussions, but I sensed a measure of prurience in his recounting of the details of that benighted Saint and her masochistic tendencies.

Actually, I think my distaste for this nonsense goes further than my position as a recovering Catholic (*so far lapsed I'm Souchong by now,* my mother used to say), at least I'd like to think it does. Bella-Marie's story is such an old story, a woman turning tricks for a succession of men: the father she lost in childhood, the lover who abandoned her, the confessor who later took on the role of biographer. Even her Christ, who had the virtue of subsuming all the other men in her life, distilling them into one dense wafer to be taken on the tongue. Once a day or as often as needed.

What interests me in this account, despite myself, is the lack of distinction made between illness cured by the Eucharist, and illness induced by the Eucharist. As with stigmata it's not possible to tell whether the wounds are inner or outer. Not only saints defy gravity. I'm so tired tonight. Two days ago my period began, and now I bleed discreetly into dry weave and quilted cotton wool. When I was young my mother used to tell me a story of the end of the world. When this old world is all tuckered out, she would say, and ready to drop from the sky, it will be rescued by a clown. He'll balance the blue globe on *his nose, careful not to spill a drop. Toss it in the air, then catch it in his mouth, g u l p! I forget how the rest goes, something about living in the belly of a clown, earthquakes when he laughed and so forth. Even if she did call herself lapsed, my mother never stopped waiting for the world to be saved.*

Tuesday, 9 May.

I saw Donna today because her mother phoned last night to tell me something she'd "forgotten" about her daughter's early years. Her dad used to cut her open sometimes, she told me, her voice echoing a little as it does when the person speaks from a closed room. I'd asked Kennedy Desjardins innumerable questions about her daughter's life, always met with vague answers and a suspiciously frank gaze. Now she has "remembered" something, do I think it might be important? Where did he cut her? I asked carefully.

At the joins, she replied. With his X-acto knife. Wrists mainly, back of the knees, once on the thigh. When I found out I put a stop to it right away, told him to leave. She was young, but. She doesn't remember anything and I don't want to remind her.

Given her own unwillingness to remember, this last contradiction on the part of Donna's mother didn't surprise me. What made you decide to tell me? I asked, dispensing with memory once and for all. She sounded frightened when she replied. I was worried, her voice hollowed out across the line, that business with Regina worried me.

Donna knocked twice before I heard and asked her to come into my office. She smiled tentatively when she held out her wrists at my request. The marks were very faint, almost invisible unless you knew where to look. Thin bloodless scars fitted neatly inside the creases. I ran my finger gently across her wrists. How did you get those marks?

She didn't pull her hand away, she didn't flinch or startle. Her body became intermittently still, one thin leg levered on the other. If she had a tail it would have been wrapped snugly about her, only the end twitching. Those are daddy's marks, she said, where he kissed me.

Thursday, 11 May.
The door of the forest opened and a pack of wolves sidled out of the shadows. *That was a sentence from a book of fairy tales my mother used to read me. It never failed to horrify, I would imagine the wolves with their powerful shoulders leaving tracks in the snow like a row of kisses at the bottom of a love letter. Always for me these two things, love and terror, all angels terrible, all gods treacherous, and who, if I cried, would hear me among the angelic orders?*

Saturday, 13 May.
A pane of glass in one of the sheds has cracked, and Molly, who can tolerate neither ambiguity nor disrepair, has hired Geisler to replace it. I sit on the steps drinking coffee and watch him tapping the old glass, feeling intuitively along the bias for the fault, then marking it with his diamond cutter. He raps sharply on the outside until the long break,

the weight of glass settling heavily into his hands. When he finishes
I watch him gather together his mallet and chisel, his collection of
blades. We use the same instruments to repair glass as to break it.

In Molly's front yard, full of the sweet-smelling flowers of early
spring for which I, being deciduous, have no name, I remember
suddenly my grandmother's garden, where three bushes met (lilac,
lemon, and something fragrant, with purple and white flowers) and
where I, coincidentally, grew up. I've given up on first causes. It is no
longer possible to say t h i s because of t h a t. I want to take Donna's
lovely, tender, listening face into my hands, say, y o u   m u s t   l o v e
n o t h i n g,   y o u   m u s t   f l e e   s o m e t h i n g. Already I see that
indigent cast about her mouth that I recognize so well, w h y   c a n ' t
y o u   b e l i e v e   h o w   m u c h   I   d o n ' t   r e m e m b e r?

In any case I wouldn't be so foolish as to force her pale face into a
confrontation with that other time. Even I can't bring myself to believe
the stigmata is the result of past abuse, blood calling to blood, the body
sloughing off its shame in accountable delirium. On the one hand,
her mimicry of the past has taken place without conscious knowledge.
On the other hand, I'm certain Donna Desjardins is no medieval
mystic fainting and burning before an obscure flame. Her body gives
off no heat other than its own healthy instincts, its will to happiness.

Meanwhile the town is reeling with the news of Regina Arnott's
blood miracle. Despite Father Ricci's dispatches to the contrary, most
people seem bent on believing otherwise. There's a certain cachet, I
suppose, about a town capable of producing not one but two stigmatics

a year, along with the usual crop of cattle feed and potatoes. Of course there are those weathered skeptics—like Molly, like Geisler—after my own heart, who tut briskly and quote old-fashioned sampler phrases like the one about idle hands and the devil's workshop.

But mostly the local curiosity that remained just this side of derision in the case of Donna has turned to devotion and a sort of communal smugness. The faces of people you pass in the street are rapt, their heads cocked as if listening to a struck chord somewhere beyond normal pitch. Hysteria has unrolled like a tarpaulin. I heard that woman from the Number Eight, Delma I think her name is, talking to the pharmacist. It stands to reason, she was saying, this town's been chosen. We all knew that Desjardins girl was special, and now Regina. She cured my auntie of varicose veins when the doctors gave up on her and she's a history of the rapture in her family, so I heard. It seems that Donna in all her innocence and now, with considerable more artifice, Regina Arnott, have been taken over as communal icons.

Worst of all, Lillian Mullen from up Fisher Branch way spread the word that she saw a small plaster statue of the Madonna moving, and now there is a constant vigil on the grass escarpment of Our Lady of Perpetual Mercy and All Saints Catholic Church. The statue is small and poorly illuminated by a halo of light bulbs. Every evening there is quite a crowd at the grotto, Protestants and Catholics alike. People stand in the twilight, murmuring the rosary and waiting to see her move. Of course the newspapers are out in force. M a d o n n a
M a n i a, they call it in four inch black letters, editorials written daily

in which adjectives like "miraculous," "hysterical" and "apocalyptic"
are used, interchangeably and without irony.

So far there've been no movements to which everyone has been
witness at the same time, but most people see movement at some point,
the end of her cloak billowing out, a tear welling from the corner of her
eye. Every now and then the curtains of the rectory twitch with agitated
weariness. Father Ricci is taking all this tribute to his church very badly.
Perhaps he suffers from an inner stigmata, a hand pressed patiently
to his side, a shortness of breath, a tendency to grimace when no-one
is looking. His statements to the Press are a wonder of nicely judged
catechism mixed with perversity. I think she can work miracles, he told
one journalist, in fact I have no doubt she can. But to me she has not
done so yet. Meanwhile it is spring, trees are turning green and mortal.

Monday, 15 May.
Went into town today to cash a cheque and bumped into Guy Turkle
at the pharmacy. He had an envelope of developed photographs from
a roll of film that Daniel Halpern gave him when he was in town last
week. Presumably he'd forgotten to collect them before he left for the
city and now Turkle wasn't sure where to send them. As always in this
town, when someone is not sure what to do they consult a professional.
A doctor will do just as well as a lawyer, and either might be eclipsed
by the dentist should he be more conveniently situated. On an impulse
I took charge of the packet, I'd seen Halpern from the corner of my eye
these last few days, lurking about the grotto and the church yard,

truffling, like his colleagues, for the dark mushroom scent of news.

When I got home I sat down and deliberately broke the seal on the envelope. I am not a woman who lives in ignorance of her motives. I have not, I flatter myself, led an unexamined life. There is something about Halpern that intrigues me, without in the least approximating on my part either sexual or romantic desire. Devout without being religious, he exudes a secular asceticism, some parasitic sorrow that has so long been private that it's no longer apparent even to its host. What's more, I disliked speaking into that tape recorder of his. He reminds me of that charlatan Honeycombe, taking down other people's stories and touting them abroad as his own.

The photographs were well taken, black and white paradigms of prairie life: a couple of abstract railway lines veering out of their own trajectory, a church steeple chill against banked clouds, an altarpiece haunted by the thin flare of a light source beyond the frame. This last especially interested me, for the impression created, no doubt accidentally, of an aura hovering above the altar. I remembered Donna saying she'd seen something like this when she first entered the church on Good Friday morning. Across the left hand corner of the photograph the developer had pasted a small sticker reading "over-exposure, suggest you check your negatives."

Thursday, 18 May.
I was standing in the check-out line at Foodtown this evening, when I saw the headline of the latest National Inquirer. *"Woman*

Gives Birth to Human Soul Weighing Two Thirds of an Ounce!" it
read. Tired and hungry, I was not in the mood for new arguments
in favour of the material continuity of life after death. I averted my
eyes and in so doing caught Daniel Halpern's. He was in the other
line, holding a pint of milk and a bag of apples. He looked tired,
diminished. Although I have thought harshly of him, the truth is I
quite like the man and was sorry to see him so gnawed about the edges.
I suspect the miraculous is getting to him, he can't be a man with
much of an appetite for excess. So I gave him my best quarter-pounder
smile and fished up his photographs from the bottom of my shoulder
bag. One day we'll look back on all this and laugh, I told him. Besides,
a hundred years from now, who's going to care? He smiled gratefully
and went on his way, a happier man, I daresay.

Saturday, 20 May.
"And things aren't just happening here. In Yorkton, Saskatchewan
there's a statue changing colour and up in Churchill there's an icon
bleeding like sweat. Down in Arizona they're having apparitions
and in Oklahoma and South Dakota and Alberta, up and down the
heartlands, statues weeping as if they were flesh and blood."

Or words to that effect. I'd gone to visit Regina Arnott because
Father Ricci called and asked me to pay a house visit. He was worried
about her health, and although she had stopped bleeding, she was a
great force in the town's religious revival. Try and get her to see reason,
he begged, his voice sidling helplessly over the line, I certainly can't.

I had no intention whatsoever of curing Regina, but I'll admit I was curious. She was noncommittal, standing aside so that I could enter her trailer and waving me to a loosely sprung chesterfield. Everything in the room—the fabric of the drapes, the rug at my feet, the faded wallpaper—had the puzzled aspect of objects that have come down in the world without knowing how.

About the room, in odd corners, were miniature shrines and grottos. One held a plaster cast of a rather conventional mother with a fluctuating smile holding out a plaster child so smooth and seamless as to appear positively deboned. Another held a life-size cardboard male figure with accusatory blue eyes, pointing heavenwards. In the far corner a crèche with a baby doll swathed in a pink blanket lay unattended by any but the most mulish of animals. A couple of candles in glass votives sputtered vaguely.

Regina was helpful in a distracted sort of way, answering questions—yes she was eating, sleeping, no there was no further pain in her wrists—with one ear cocked for communication from the other world. She would stop talking, listen, pause, then continue with an ever more distracted glaze to her arctic eyes.

In her case I don't hesitate to speculate that the apparitions with which she surrounded herself, the Madonna and Child, Christ the King, and Baby Jesus, formed a substitute for her own unholy family. Outside a brimming moon poured into the room.

Do you notice how many women in this town wear gloves? she asked inconsequentially. There's the church ladies, the nurses at the hospital, and of course, everyone wears mittens in winter. Why, even Molly Rhutabaga wears gardening gloves most of the time, but I mustn't gossip.

And she cast a glance of exaggerated concern towards the upright figure of Jesus Christ who seemed to be monumentally oblivious, engaged as he was in giving the finger to heaven. He hears everything I say, she told me, and I'm under special orders this week to practice charity in everything I do. There now, you've started the baby crying!

She moved rapidly across the room, picked up the doll from its cradle, pressing it to her breast and murmuring endearments. Did you know, she looked up briefly, the last person to touch that blessed Donna before she bled was her mother? Oh, and while I'm on the subject, ask Geisler why he never takes off his shoes in public.

I didn't stay much longer but turned back once to wave goodbye. Regina was standing at the window, the doll held tightly in her arms. Her face had grown soft, as if catching the wings in passing of one of Rilke's terrible, beautiful angels, serenely disdaining to destroy.

Sunday, 21 May.

I once attended an international medical conference for women. We all spoke different languages, couldn't understand one another. Until, that is, we put on headphones and simultaneous translation began. Then we debated, argued, made resolutions, and took down decisions in a fluent, generous currency that had each of us believing the other women had magically learnt our own language. Of course, as soon as *we took off the headphones and left the room we were at a loss with one another.*

That's how I feel about Bella-Marie Lambe-of-God. As if her voice has been drawn out of her mouth in a long thread and cropped into prim black marks on a page. When the book opens I understand her, but when it closes we're strangers. Her voice tracks white noise or the tympanic emptiness of a seashell, only it's not Bella-Marie who speaks, it never was. It's that Patron Saint of Hysteria, that old Honeycomber, that priestly devil with moveable mouth-parts who perches on her arm and talks for her.

Tuesday, 23 May.

Had a strange dream about Daniel Halpern last night. We were standing together on the Number 8 highway next to the body of a cat some careless motorist had sideswiped and left for dead. The cat was crushed against the hot tar, bleeding copiously. I was terribly upset, tottering in precarious circles around her, and trying to staunch the blood with my palms. For some reason I was searching for a synonym for the word red, I'd got it into my head that if I could describe the colour of the blood it would begin to clot.

I remember kneeling at the side of the road, feeling the sharp gravel against my knees, murmuring s c a r l e t, c r i m s o n, v e r m i l i o n, whispering r o s e, b r i c k, r u s t. Halpern moved forward, put his hands on my shoulders, I know a little about cats, he said, although less, surely, than they know of us.

At these words I began to cry inconsolably, the tears running down my cheeks and mingling with the cat's blood. Ssh, he said, kneeling beside me and patting my back with enormous gentleness, hush, h u s h. I recall we stayed that way for some time.

Gentle Reader,

It would please me so much to report that Daniel and Virginie became lovers. He with his reluctant body, she with her carnivorous mouth. Imagine it is the end of summer— three, four red moons have come and gone. The last reporters have left town, the church and its grounds are being cleared of the accumulated detritus of unbelief. Massimo sits alone in his study indulging in one of his gorgeous rages, peacock and paisley in colour, righteous in intent. At the Care Home, the patients are being prepared for their afternoon amble. A nurse makes a note to herself to clean out the Isaacs room. Away in the city, that poisonous creature, that autodidact of a curator, Dr. Helena Skuros, is surreptitiously reading the dictionary beneath her bed covers. She balances the book on her knees and one hand holds a flashlight, but the other hand, the willful hand, is busy elsewhere.

In the Desjardins household, unhaunted now by any but the

most domestically inclined of spirits, Donna is watching the television antics of a cartoon mouse. She is wondering what came first, history or the Bible stories that have for so long fixed her life like a solvent. In another room her brother is changing gears, but quietly, gently, to keep from waking the baby that sleeps overhead. And Regina? Sedate, sedated, she bends over a bush opulent with wild roses, her secateurs poised.

Imagine all this and then imagine the telephone ringing in the evening silence of Virginie's log cabin. *Hello*, he says, and yes of course she shouldn't have given her number to a journalist, do you think she hasn't reproached herself for that already? At once he begins to murmur into the crisp conch of her ear. When she recalls this moment it will have all the resonance of impli-cation, the means by which we surmount death through perfect love, or at least through the memory of its perfection. As for Halpern, he will forget this moment immediately so as to be able to remember it later, freeze-dried in the past tense.

The first part of their romance will be made up of recollections of the older woman, landlady to one, confidante to both. They will speak of my luminous eccentricities, my name like a root vegetable, my preoccupation with memory and its discords. Soon they will realize that from their common past they have established an uncommon present, amber already staining the fluctuating trace of his voice on the telephone line. Sluggish and snail-hungry, love will salt them down in the end, after the final betrayal. After the wine, the cheese served at room temperature, the smoked mussels. After the word *always*, after Rilke's second elegy. A kiss like a brass rubbing reversed upon the lips of the other.

We are approaching the end of the story. I will not be with you much longer, and loitering is a dangerous practice in a world divided by innocence and experience, innocence and guilt. If my story were really about Halpern and Virginie, such an ending would be *de rigeur*. As it is, as by now I'm sure you will have guessed, I'm a poor reader of my own writing. Halpern huddled over his terrible pity like some fruit rotting from the inside out, Ginny (my sweet girl) flaunting her solitude like a rebellious act. A union between those two would be so unlikely that it will not be referred to again, except by omission. Instead, I have to accomplish a movement from the metaphorical to the physical world, a second fall, this time into grace.

Imagine tomatoes blowing from the vine, fully dilated. The carrots you planted in early spring are already so thick with foreknowledge they have pushed the earth into ridges of knuckle. Strawberries, raspberries, chokecherries droop heavily from their bushes, whispering *sugar, sugar*. Rows of corn creak in their secret husks, rehearsing the incalculable longings of vegetable matter. In the forked branches of trees, crabapples and pears fatten between leaves while beneath them in the earth, tubers root, undertaking their own horticultural inquiry. Even the seed catalogues have begun to sprout this year, putting out tendrils and roots in locked drawers. This unseasonal variety, this unnatural abundance of growing things all ripening together, provide a context for our lapse, before which we lived in a state of grace uncomplicated by desire or obedience.

Beyond the garden I sit at the window, the joints of my fingers so twisted with arthritis that my hands seem to offer themselves to prayer. Like the earth, the body represents what it cannot have. There's not much time left. I am wearing the eye glasses that Virginie's father gave me before he died. They are the wrong prescription but there is very little left that I wish to see. I've asked Regina to put a record on the stereo and the opening phrase of one of Beethoven's last string quartets circles taut and resinous about these rooms, pulling us through the last hours of daylight with rosin on our fingertips. I like listening to music by a man so overcome by sacrifice that he did not suffer to hear his own compositions. And you, gentle reader, are you quite comfortable?

THE KITCHENMAID'S TALE

n the town of Chepstow on the Wye was a castle built on a hill where lived for many years a lord and his family. My sisters told me that when I was of thirteen years I could go to work at the castle as a kitchen maid, this they told me at eleven and at twelve. My oldest sister was already of this age and when she came back from the castle at evening she would sit with us upon a bank and tell of the wonders that she saw within. Of the candles of wax and tallow supported on wall brackets and iron candelabra. Of the huge fireplace and hearth with a *couvre-feu* of Chinese tile and of the murals of finest linen and green wool spangled with silver profiles of men and women. Of the floors strewn with rushes and herbs, basil, balm, chamomile, costmary, cowslip, sweet fennel, hyssop, lavender, marjoram, mint, tansy and winter savoury.

From that day when Antropine, my oldest sister, first went to work at the Castle, she stopped being a mother to us and since we had no other, we could no longer remain children. Instead we grew up, quick as broad-beans, with a tuck and a seam and our hair taken up and fastened with combs of ivory. We had beautiful hair, we three, hanging like shawls of Spanish lace down our backs. My second sister, Digitalis, and I spent the days of the summer solstice weaving our hair into braids while Antropine went off early in the morning to the gates of the Castle. At night she would come home and sit wearily in a corner of the room, her eyes closed covetously on a vision that even we, her two beloved sisters, could not share. One day, she would say at these times, you will go to the Castle also. Meanwhile, I grew my hair and waited.

Our mother was a water dowser, who used to travel through all the county listening for the sound of water moving like shot silk beneath the earth. No rain for years at a time then as now, and so the townspeople waited anxiously for the dowser. One night, long ago, she came to my father's house weeping. She had been stung, she told him, by a dark red scorpion whilst out in the fields that day. The pain, oh the pain was unbearable, he must help her, and she sank in a heap on his doorstep, wet and slick with sweat and fear. My father was the town apothecary who had in the absence of a doctor become skilled in the arts of healing, and he gathered her in his faithful arms and laid her upon his bed. Then he went back to the door and shut it firmly against the eyes of the townspeople straining through the darkness. Oh foolish father! You should not, you really should not have shut that door. My father is—was—no *is*, a kind and generous man. He wanted to shield the water-dowser from the speculation of his neighbours and the scandal of the night. But he should never have shut the door.

Inside, the water-dowser stirred and moaned. Her eyes fluttered against the light and her curved nostrils flared wide. Where is the sting, asked my father, my foolish father. She gestured to a place on her upper thigh and rolled her eyes and panted. My father hastily untied her skirt and bent a little closer. Quick as knives she was up and on him. She wrestled him down and onto the floor and she twined those polished thighs about his waist and took him where he lay, my fond and foolish father.

The townspeople say she poisoned him that day, striking into the soft flesh of his belly with her dark pincers. For my father was poisoned, at any rate he fell in love as others fall to sin, and grew ill with the effects. I say she only wanted a baby, and diviner that she was could hear the seed moving in my father as easily as she could hear water flowing beneath the earth.

And she did fall to child, my mother the water-dowser, who left my father that very night for a distant town where water was scarce, oh scarcer even than here. He never saw her for twelve months and he grew thin and whittled, a winter branch in the wind. He took to walking through the night, gazing up towards the northern cross that blazed beyond his reach on the horizon.

Then one day my mother walked into town. She carried, so they say, a forked willow branch in one hand and an infant in the other. She walked through the town and into his house with a distracted expression as if her mind were on other worlds. The apothecary opened his door to let the water-dowser through and once more closed it on the raking stares of the townsfolk.

Those were not easy times. That night the people of the town stormed the house of the apothecary, demanding that he give the dowser into their hands. Of course it was the season of rain, and memory had failed them. They could not conceive of a time when she would be of use to them. But the woman who was to become my mother had already left, off on her journey again, forked willow branch pointed at the earth, forked eyes fixed on the sky. She left the infant with my father in recompense for her absence, all to the good since she already had the start of another lodged cozily in the side of her precious womb.

Two times more she came and went, riffling each time the tender heart of the apothecary, first with her absence, then with her presence, then with her absence again. My father was left with three nameless daughters and he called us Antropine, Digitalis and Belladonna. We were his three droplets of venom in memory of the woman who had turned on him like a scorpion and poisoned him with her blood.

So my father brought us up in his fond, foolish way, without wife, without mother, without even the patronage of the townsfolk for whom we were less than fowl dropping. But not alas, without the presence of Beatrice, my mother's mother, who came one day, a battered crone, to beg for alms and a home in my father's house. Her flesh was ashen and dry as coal dust, she pecked each one of us on the cheek with a kiss like pinched flesh. Of course my father took her in.

Now that he had provided us with a mother, he was able to relieve us of a father. After apprenticing each one of us as kitchenmaids to the family at the Castle on the Wye, he packed a traveling bag with ointments and unguents, balms and pastes, and took off to look for his antidote. He would support himself by ministering to the sick and faithless in the towns he passed through whilst looking for his beloved who listened only for the water that gushed beneath the earth, not for the weary footsteps of my lovesick papa.

As for Grandmother Beatrice, she took to her room with alacrity and rarely left it in the years that followed. We would bring porridge and milk to her door, shying away from the ragged fingers that came sidling forward to grasp the bowl and the sudden twist of tarnished breath that seeped at us as she cackled her thanks. Meanwhile time passed. I listened for the trapped gurgle of water beneath the earth but could hear nothing. I grew my hair and waited.

Presently it was the thirteenth birthday of my sister Digitalis, and she set off early to the gates of the Castle. In the evening she sat with Antropine and I, and told of the wonders within. Of the bailey near the kitchen where fruit trees and vines grew, also potted herbs and flowers. Of the roses, lilies, heliotropes, violets, poppies, daffodils, iris and gladioli that clustered near the north wall. Of the fishponds stocked with pike and trout and the cellar built far beneath the earth and filled with barrels of pale green wine.

And my sister shuddered once and closed her greedy eyes and the northern stars blazed suddenly into the night. I was alone after that, and grew weary of growing my hair. I took to whiling time, a skein of wool about my wrist, in the company of my grandmother. She would rock slowly before me on her lean haunches, insert her finger between a ribcage thin and wrung as a washing board. Such tales she told, tales that I have long forgotten and could not repeat. Until I turned thirteen and was sent on my way to the Castle.

Now the three of us sat on the riverbank as evening fell, but I could see nothing of my sisters for the light that burned through the sockets of my eyes. I could see nothing but the curve of a cheek that had been turned away from me at dinner, and the length of a forearm veined and sown with a scattered crop of wheatblond hairs. I tried to describe to my sisters the beauty of that arm, the charm of that half-turned cheek flushed with food and good humour. But when they learnt to whom it belonged, they threw their aprons over their heads and rocked backwards and forwards crying, *no good can come of this, no good, no good.*

To love is to crave the proximity of objects. The porcelain bowl of half-eaten porridge that he had flooded in clotted cream and skinned with heaps of coarse sugar was dearer to me than my own pink heart. I put the spoon to my mouth and soon had eaten all the cold mess of his leavings.

I found him one day, this youngest son, asleep in the orchard where he had been reading a book of courtly lays. I drew closer and thoughtlessly moved to pluck from his hand the half eaten apple that still bore the imprint of his teeth. It was then that I saw the scorpion sting at the base of his wrist.

If I had known his cousin, with skin like double cream and lips more vermeil than rose or cherry, was in the orchard that morning, and that when he awoke, the first thing he would see would be her face above his, if I had known he would look at her and be struck down by love, perhaps I would never have put my hot, loving mouth to his wrist and sucked the poison out of him and into me.

There was to be a grand party at the Castle, a plighting of troths to celebrate the marriage of two great houses. A lowly kitchenmaid I was not invited, although I had saved the young master from certain death for certain prosperity. On the day of the wedding party at the Castle, the air was cider, the fields smelled of warm wheat and the sun was a gently steaming yolk, a new-laid egg in the sky. I was called into the morning chamber so that the young Lord and his betrothed could properly thank me. She slipped her narrow hand into his broad one as if to demonstrate what was evident. You have saved him so that I may spend him.

I went to Beatrice. Can you give me poison, my grandmother? She let out a cackle and rubbed the palms of her old hands together with the tight squeak of leather. That night I cut at my braids, snipping them off one by one. They fell to the floor like oiled threads. I gathered them up and wove them into a knot of gleaming plumage and took it to my grandmother. In return she handed me a jar covered with cheesecloth. Antropine and Digitalis watched in silence but with my new knowledge I could hear the words of their thoughts, *no good can come of this, no good, no good!*

I carried my jar carefully down stairs, across fields, under stars, through the gate and into the castle where, in the second floor chamber lay my love with his love. I was my mother's daughter, I would poison them both with the scorpion I carried, pickled in amber to preserve its strength. Through the hall and past the first of the great bed chambers, a passage opened into the nave of the chapel where a light shone constantly above the altar. And in this quiet place I knew that I could not kill the man I had loved and saved and lost. I could not kill her whom he loved. Perhaps I was my father's daughter after all.

It was then I fell upon my knees in the chapel before the shrine of Our Lady of Mercy and begged for what it was her name promised. Once I could have been like cold ale, full of froth and bubble, men could have drunk me up and been all the stronger for it. Once I thought to plunge my own hand into the jar and fish out the bloody fang, the scorpion who was also my mother, and put her to my lips.

Then it was that I lost the world and lay all night at the foot of the cross, and a vision came to me of Our Lord with his hair thick and gold upon his brow. My Lord looked down upon me with the beloved face of my lord. The wound upon his breast flowed with blood, but to me, so parched and hungry, it seemed that a voice from above bid me drink from the breast that would nourish my holy infancy. And when I put up my mouth to obey, it was milk that flowed down my throat, milk rich and sweet, to feed my body, my soul. And I felt such maternal desire for Him, such spousal love, that my flesh became His flesh, my body His body. Like Him I could be hurt, like Him I had suffered, bled. Thus it was that this Father with souls lodged in His womb gave birth to me. A voice from the altar commanded, *Hasten to the Convent at Basel and there join yourself to your true sisters so that their mouths can conceive breath from yours.*

And this I did.

O Lord, our Lord, how marvelous Thy name, spread through the reaches of the earth! Wherefore in honour of Thee, as best I can I tell my tale. Guide Thou the song that I have sung for Thee!

At the convent in Basel I was welcomed by many and by many shown the way. First there was the good sister Lukardis of Ghent who grew so agitated in her mind when she recalled the suffering of our Lord, how nails were hammered into His palms, that she would strike violently with the tip of her finger pointed like a nail, at the same place upon her own hand until she drew blood. Father Thomas Honeycombe who consents to hear our confessions in this place, declared upon examining the finger that it had the hardness of metal and was altogether without the tactility of flesh. With this same finger, at the hours of Sext and None, she strikes herself violently upon the breast with a sound that is like the ring of a hammer falling on the head of a nail. The noise echoes throughout the convent at these hours, and we find her to be more trustworthy than the bells.

Others of us refuse to eat, like Sister Margaret, who pokes sticks down her throat so that she may bring up the food she cannot bear in her stomach. These days she will take only the Eucharist, which she chews minutely, for she reckons precisely how many souls God will permit her to remove from purgatory by the number of crumbs into which she has chewed the host. Father Honeycombe holds her up as a model of daintiness. In Sister Margaret, he says, we find the horror of corporeality that is truly Divine. No, good sir, I overheard the Prioress contradict him, hers is not a rooting out of the physical but a quest for what is truly nourishing: the flesh of our Lord chewed and swallowed, delicious, Divine.

And still others of us simply become the flesh of Christ our Lord, because our flesh can do what his could do. Like him we feed and bleed, like him we die, and in dying, we give life to others. There is a story of a scribe who patiently copied out many holy books in his life. He died, and over time his body turned to dust but his right hand, his scribe's hand, was found many years later, supple and undecayed. For you see, if once you have touched something that is holy, you have been yourself touched, holiness enters your body and cannot be renounced. Therefore, Lord, as you will, so may it be. Amen. ❦

Virginie's Confession

W h e n Virginie contacted the newspaper where Daniel Halpern worked she learned he was on sick-leave. She told the receptionist she was a doctor and anxious to get in touch with him, and was given his home address where he was convalescing after an operation to remove a tumor on his liver. She phoned and his voice on the line was pale and strained as if he were trying to speak without drawing breath, but he was perfectly hospitable. "Yes, yes, come over by all means," he told her. "Whenever you're in the city. You don't need to call first, I'm not going anywhere."

But she did call, a week ago, to be exact. She took him a bunch of hot-house grapes and a jar of early spring daffodils because she often saw such things on the bedside tables of patients recovering from surgery. Daniel opened the door himself, walking cautiously, the way convalescents who are trying to grow into their newly partitioned bodies do. He had the bewildered look of those who have suffered unexpected physical duress after a life that has neglected to prepare them for pain. But he was glad to see Virginie, she could tell by the way he shuffled into the kitchen to switch on the kettle and by the effort he had made to dress in a shirt and trousers for her visit.

It was the first tolerably mild day of spring and they sat at the open door to his balcony. He lived on the top floor of a high-rise apartment block overlooking the Assiniboine River where the gulls came and went after the ice had broken. At first they spoke of his surgery. The tumor was benign but had grown at an alarming rate so that, along with a good chunk of liver, two ribs from his diaphragm had been removed. He was still unable to stand upright or lift objects, or even to breathe with ease, but he had spent the winter "trying to fatten my liver," he told her, "like some anaemic Strasbourg goose."

Virginie suddenly remembered the first time she met him, when he'd come to the hospital to interview her, and how distraught she'd been, although she'd tried to hide it. She was unnerved at the blood-miracle that had occurred and at her inability to staunch that wound.

Daniel seemed to be remembering the same time because he looked at her suddenly, not as he had been, with courtesy and mild interest, but with directness. She saw how his eyes had sunk into their fallen flesh, giving him a sort of bruised intensity. "How's the unicorn-girl?" he asked, but he did not mean it facetiously and Virginie was happy to report that she was mortal again.

Then the kettle whistled and she busied herself pouring some kind of herbal extract into the cups and saucers he laid out, and while she was mashing the last of the tea-bags into hot water she saw a way to introduce the subject she'd come so far to discuss. "Remember how Molly insisted on real loose-leaf tea brewed for exactly four minutes in a heated tea-pot?" she asked, handing him his cup. He didn't reply, except that his hands shook a little and some tea slopped into the saucer. The anesthetic and the long months of recovery had weakened him. They sat in silence for some minutes as he swallow-swallowed and blinked the water from his eyes.

When Daniel recovered, he began to talk about Molly, and Virginie saw that their friendship had been one of equals, not, as in her case, the respect accorded to an older woman by a younger woman.

"I couldn't get to the funeral," he said, gesturing at his concave chest, "but I thought about her all that day. How she was finally being planted in the earth after all those years of planting other things; seeds and bulbs, flags and fence-posts, vegetables. That night I dreamed orchids began to grow from her open mouth, her eye-sockets. For months after I was afraid to close my eyes. And then one night it simply lost its power. There she was, planted in the earth, dying and flowering, and I thought, how lovely, and after that I never had the dream again. Or if I did, I've forgotten it.

"She was so *fastidious*, and when I read how she died—the newspapers called it a blood-bath—I thought chaos is come again, and then that perhaps it was a blessing. I mean never having to grow feeble in old age, and then I don't know what I thought because the pain was more or less constant and I had to learn to breathe through it, there wasn't room for anything else. Sometimes, at night when there was nobody to call, I imagined her sitting up with me the way we used to, the smoke from her cigar blowing through the window pane and into the night. I don't mean I felt her presence in the way people say, the ones who claim to be talking with angels. No, it was just pain and confusion on my part, smoke and the wind on hers.

"And then I began to feel guilty. All those papers I gave her, the interviews and work-notes. You might not know about those. Anyway, at one point I thought they might have had something to do with her death. You have to remember I was very weak at the time and the past kept lurching into the present. I thought perhaps—well you see, I still don't understand."

He trailed off and was gazing into the middle distance where the river cut away from its course into a banked curve. Two children had come down to the edge and were throwing stones into the current. A season ago Virginie would have worried that one or both would fall into the icy water, perhaps drown. She would have shouted to them to stand back, or warned them of the dangers of melting ice. Now she knew there was little she could do to protect herself, let alone others, and she merely closed the window because Daniel seemed unaware that the air had grown colder.

"Molly was having tea at her kitchen table when she was attacked," she reassured him, "I don't believe anyone else was aware of your files or had any feeling about their significance. What else don't you understand?" The question was kindly meant but inadequate. She knew from experience that the weight of what he understood could never tip over what remained inexplicable. But she had come, she thought ironically, as a healer, to offer him words from her limited store of reassurances. Because he had been ill when Molly died, and because he was the only other person who had loved her with something like equality.

"I hardly know where to begin. After Molly died I worked double shifts at the hospital, then walked for hours every evening along the highway to tire myself out so that I would sleep dreamlessly. A niece from Ontario came to pack up what I believe were called her *effects*, and much of the furniture was sold at the Interlake Auction that Fall."

"I didn't know there was a niece, what's she like?"

"Nice enough, even sorry in a perfunctory sort of way, for what she called the *tragic circumstances* of her aunt's passing. She wore a cardigan, the limp sleeves rolled up to her elbows and spoke in italics, every now and then emphasizing a phrase so that it was all I could do not to point out that Auntie Molly, as she persisted in calling her, had not so much *passed over* as been *unseemly thrust*. But it didn't seem necessary to dwell on the semantic irregularities of Molly's death since her niece did not pretend to any great loss, and I was grateful for that."

Instead, Virginie had become obsessed with the word *tragic*, the word everyone was to use, first at the funeral and later, for what seemed like weeks, in the newspapers, until the first snowfall of the year broke all records and the gossip that bobbed along in the wake of Molly's death gave way to the more pressing concerns of digging themselves out from beneath three feet of wet snow.

Daniel shifted slightly, "You found her?"

Virginie, who had found Molly on her kitchen floor, her throat neatly snipped and gaping open, her face blooming blood like the petals on some carefully reared prize rose bush, said nothing.

"Christ, you must have been shocked!"

"Shocked, yes, and frightened, all the while that I shooed Franklin from the room. You can still see the paw prints he made at the edges of the rug after sliding in her blood."

"What did you do?"

"Phoned the RCMP, then ran to the front gate to let them in. The officer in charge was called Fisher. He sat in my living room, thick and burly with a crease down the centre of his trousers and another across the width of his brow. He was very kind, reassuring me that I was quite safe, even going into my kitchen and boiling the kettle for a cup of tea. I didn't know the police did that. When he came back, he set the cup down at my elbow and began to stir rapidly with a teaspoon."

The sight of his hands clasped awkwardly about the fragile cup had made her laugh and then—horribly, shamefully —cry. Fisher had seemed unsurprised by her reaction and lifted the cup to her mouth so she was forced to drink. The tea was dense with sweetness, and soon she was able to "sit up and talk" as her mother would have said.

"Did he suspect you?"

"We all of us knew to a certainty who had killed Molly. It only remained for me to tell my story so that, as Fisher put it, we could close the file and get on with our lives. What made you look in on her? he asked, to get me started.

"When I came back from the hospital that night the house was quite dark. That was unusual as Molly was in the habit of leaving her porch light on, but I thought nothing of it at the time, I was very tired and went straight to bed. I woke early because Franklin was barking outside my window. Molly was nowhere to be seen but I assumed she was somewhere on the property, just out of sight, seeing to her late season's corn. In an adjacent field the men were tending to the last of the alfalfa crop, rolling the springy stuff into bales for cattle-feed. The sky was high, the wind abrupt, what Molly would have called 'nip and tuck weather' and I remember locking the door, then going back into the cabin for my gloves.

"I spent the whole day at the hospital. One of my mothers broke water around noon and she had a difficult delivery. It was just after six when I got home to an empty house and a sink full of dirty water. Quite automatically, I imagine, because I certainly don't remember doing it, I moved to the faucet and began to rinse the stacked dishes."

It was then, her hands drifting in warm water, that she looked across the lawn towards Molly's house. The farmhouse had an uncharacteristically shuttered look, the windows closed and the drift of leaves that had fallen on her stairs overnight not swept away. Although it was almost dark, no lights were on and Franklin had dragged what looked like a large bath towel from the washing line and torn it to rags. He lay now in one of Molly's careful flower beds gnawing at a piece of fabric and looking at once morose and woebegone. Virginie did not remember crossing the lawn or opening the front door. She knew she hadn't stopped to put on her boots because her feet, when she finally remembered them, were icy and remained so all that long night.

"The RCMP were decisive and efficient. Fisher took me back to my cabin—I'd begun to shake—and a police car remained alongside the house all night. Shortly before dawn, Regina was picked up on the highway to Thompson. She'd hitchhiked some two hundred kilometres north and was soaking wet with rain, sweat, and a can of beer she'd spilt over the front of her shirt and because of which had been ignominiously turned out on the edge of the highway by a trucker more fastidious than most. The baby Christ doll she'd once proudly shown me was huddled beneath her jacket, and her eyes, Fisher tells me, were dilated and ecstatic. His word, *ecstatic.*"

"I still can't believe it! How—what did she look like?" Daniel's face had drained, Virginie poured him another cup of tea but did not stop talking.

"Molly was lying on her back with her arms flung out, her hands open, and one foot bent beneath her. There was a smell in the air of something dense, of fish gutted on a wet dock or game hung up to cure and ripen. I remember the taste of rust, like decayed iron, in my mouth and a single mechanical rasp repeated over and over in the banked shadows. Later I learned this was the needle of the record player that had pulled back and was catching on air. The record was a late string quartet by Beethoven.

"All of this is memory in retrospect. What I was aware of immediately and then overwhelmingly, was the blood. There was blood on every surface, smeared thin as a wash of water colour or thickly layered in heavy impasto. The blood stained the kitchen tiles and coagulated in a pot of chicken soup on the stove, the blood had soaked into the rug and transformed the cabbage roses on the drapes. As for her face, Molly's face, it was quite obscured."

"*Who would have thought the old woman to have had so much blood!*"

"Interesting you should say that. I once confided to Molly a dream I had about a cat dying on the highway. I knew I could save the cat's life if I named the precise colour of the blood running in rivulets from the poor animal. Talk about the inadequacy of life compared to art! I stood over the dead body of a woman whom—if I didn't know it then, I surely did later—I had loved, and I certainly did not quote Lady Macbeth."

Nor had she tried to name the colours of Molly's glorious and pungent cloak, nor did she, then or ever after, feel pity or terror. She stood looking down at Molly and her glance had already turned diagnostic.

"When the carotid artery is severed, as Molly's was, with an instrument that was later identified as a pair of common garden secateurs, the trajectory of the blood is high and wide, accounting for the splashes on the walls and drapes, traces of blood as high as the ceiling. Death is almost instantaneous, occasioned by loss of blood, not to mention shock. Most frequently the victim is unaware of what's happened. When the RCMP arrived they cordoned off the area, then sent to the hospital for a doctor, since death has to be medically established, no matter how obvious it appears to the layman."

With what could only be described as exquisite irony, the hospital had paged Virginie to let her know that her expertise was needed on the Rhutabaga share-holding. Since Dr. Jacobs was attending an unexpected breech birth that evening, would she take over his shift? There was no other doctor in Annex. Virginie had taken brief note of Fisher's discomfort, the other RCMP officer staring at his boots with clumsy absorption. She had walked back inside, knelt at her head. Beneath the mask of blood, Molly was wearing a pair of glasses she'd never seen before, but they effectively shielded the upper part of her face so that suddenly, unexpectedly, she was gazing into her clear, shocked eyes. Molly's eyes.

Daniel had been straining forward as she spoke but on the last words he exhaled, sank back. "You know, when I heard how she died I was *relieved*. I mean because she'd been murdered and not spirited away."

"I know what you mean. There's just so much mysterious blood one can take before one begins, perversely, to long for the ordinary kind. Three weeks ago I looked up the entry under *Blood* in my medical encyclopedia. I didn't expect to learn anything new, it's just that I've been surrounded by blood for so long now that I thought to end the subject once and for all with a good, dry read."

For a long time she had looked at a diagram of arterial circulation in the human body, the intricate tracery of capillaries, the arteries like the arching branches of a tree with their scattering of twigs and brittle arterioles. She'd had a professor once who grew quite passionate about William Harvey's demonstration of the circulation of blood in 1628. Imagine, he would say, peering at his students over the top of his bifocals, until then people believed blood was in continuous to-and-fro motion! Virginie was not sure why this sentence remained with her when she had forgotten so much else of those early years of study and sleeplessness. In view of the mysteries that plagued the town that year, it did her good to read a bracing account of the heart and its secular allegiances. The article began with the usual admonition to common-sense—The Heart is a Pump—and ended thirty-five pages later with a summary of the disorders of the pulmonary system that included anaemia, polycythemia and leukemia, but made no mention of stigmata, sainthood, or ecstasy.

Daniel shifted restlessly. "When she heard about my operation she came into town to see me and was the same sweet Molly, holding my hand as I slipped in and out of consciousness. They tell me she came two or three times but they've all dissolved in my head and it's just that once I remember, her face hanging above me. And I couldn't even go to the funeral."

"She was buried on a dreary day, and most of the town turned out to hear her eulogized because she'd been born and had lived, for most of her life, in Annex. And because of the way she died, which seemed to provide a fitting, not to say *voluptuous* finale to the season of blood-letting. I don't mean that she wasn't mourned or wouldn't be missed, because, as you know, for all her irony, Molly was a woman of generosity and many kind deeds. But the scandal of her death and the arrest a day later of Regina Arnott had much to do with the number of mourners at her funeral.

"It was held at the Methodist cemetery, and people came in their station wagons and pick-ups all the way from Hunter's Lake and Leaf Rapids. The schools and banks were closed, the flag outside the city hall building flew at half mast all day, and three minutes of silence was observed in businesses at noon.

"How Molly would have enjoyed the pageantry. I imagine her creeping into the back of the church, like Tom Sawyer, wiping a tear from her eye as her acts of generosity were lauded, smiling briefly as her eccentricities were remembered, and finally, permitting herself a moment of self-congratulation at the hundreds of people who'd gathered from all over the Interlake to see her properly buried."

Massimo Ricci had been there, looking care-worn and self-important at the same time, steering his brittle mother carefully across the gravel and nodding solemnly to those of his flock who had strayed onto Protestant ground. And the nurses at the hospital wheeling their patients from the Care Home, the church women carrying small parcels of thimble cookies and matrimonial cake for the funeral tea, even some of the school children who knew Molly through her work at the Annex Museum were there, looking stilted in their dark clothes. Virginie had seen Donna Desjardins standing on one peripatetic leg with her grandmother at the side of the hall. She waved to Virginie, a brief, open-handed young girl's greeting.

"Molly's niece descended on us a week or so after the funeral to pack up her aunt's house and get it ready for the auction. She drove down in a rented car, disappeared into the house, threw open all the windows and proceeded to clean the old farm-house within an inch of its life. Unabashedly energetic, the niece—whose name I refuse to remember—soon had the place breathing and billowing in layers of dust and time. Every now and then, Franklin and I would hear the whine of the vacuum cleaner, the thud of carpets being soundly beaten and then an exclamation of annoyance at some recalcitrant stain or other. Of course the blood had already been cleaned away by volunteers from the church but Molly was always slightly undomesticated and Regina, as we now know, had other things on her mind.

"One evening, when I came home from the hospital, the niece was waiting for me. She carried a box filled with cardboard folders and a set of bound pages which she deposited in my arms with a curdled remark about Aunt Molly's writing habit. She used the same tone of voice as she would have in announcing that Molly had been a secret drinker, the two things, no doubt in her mind, analogous.

"I found out then that Molly had left a will of some kind, informal but quite legal. I'm not sure why this surprised me.

After all, she was what you would call—if you didn't know her—an 'elderly' woman with a good business sense. It was just, I suppose, that she had very recently amended the will to the effect that I was to inherit her papers when she died. The codicil was dated three days before her death, giving the uncanny impression, as I heard Delma Thorkelson up at the Motel say, that she as good as knew something was going to happen, she could smell her death on the wind. Such ghoulish imaginings aside, I'd witnessed Molly burning piles of her papers some months before and thought that summed up her attitude to the past."

That night Virginie began to read the files, beginning with the bound pages, and all hope of sleep was lost. Over the next few weeks she methodically read the notes and interviews Daniel had transcribed, his sly jottings, and the conscientious, careful research he'd done on stigmata. Despite the haphazard manner in which they were presented, his notes were not disordered. Indeed, they looked as if they'd been arranged in chronological sequence either by himself or by Molly, who had somehow acquired his store of research.

"What made you turn over your notes to Molly anyway?"

"It was all getting too much for me. No matter which way I turned the story over in my mind, I couldn't see that any one explanation for the child's bleeding was better than another. I read and researched, I interviewed people. Everyone had his own theory but nothing made sense. I remember Ricci saying something I still don't understand. You have to live near a railway line if you want to see trains. That was it. You can't imagine how I've wrung those words for meaning. I began to see significance in everything.

"At the centre of it all a small child, wincing and bleeding. I tell you it was an outrage, what that crippled god of theirs was doing. Every night I'd sit opposite Molly and she'd ask me how things were going. But she wasn't satisfied with my anger. What do you think happened to her? she'd say. What really happened? Until I was too tired to leave and I'd fall asleep in the chair. Then she'd wake me, tell me to go to bed, but it would start all over again. Did I think it was a hoax? Why had I spoken to Mina Isaacs at the Care Home? What did I think of you?

"You have no idea how she harried me, soon it was as if all her questions entered my blood-stream. I got no peace at all, every moment strung between incredulity and disbelief and I thought I was going mad. They say it happens sometimes to reporters, burn-out or whatever. You're tired and overworked, suddenly a story snags your imagination and you become— well, obsessed I suppose."

It was growing late, the shadows lengthening from their base. Daniel was tired, he leaned his head against his arm and watched the sun churn up the setting clouds.

"It all seems so long ago. As if I were looking through long distance binoculars. One night Molly pushed me too far and I let her have it. Who did she think she was, did she imagine she could do a better job than I was, would she like to try? Yes, she said, is that a challenge?

"It was just after Regina's hoax, when the summer miracles began. I'd come back late from the Madonna vigil on the church grounds and damned if I hadn't seen that granite cloak billow out on the wind for a second. Full of self-loathing, hating myself for my gullibility, I was unable to convince myself what I'd seen had been a trick of light. Something, some strung tendon in my chest seemed to give way, the air between us grew thick and full of venom. Fine, I snapped at her, I give up. Here are my notes, we'll see what kind of job you do.

"That night I got into my car and drove all the way to the city. I've never done anything like it before or since, never lost my temper, or given up on an assignment, or deserted a friend. I drove back to Winnipeg that night with my foot flat against the floor, looking back into the rear-view mirror, I swear, more than I looked forward. The next day I began to hemorrhage internally and they rushed me to hospital and operated within the week and for months after I was lost somewhere between the devil and the frying pan. I didn't know what happened to the research notes I left with her, what she made of them."

For a moment the setting sun hung above the horizon, the room flared into fugitive light. Virginie couldn't help herself and asked him what, clearly, he had been trying to avoid answering: "What happened to make Donna bleed?"

Daniel looked out at the city spread beneath them. On either side of the river and beyond, trees and houses, streets, busses, office-blocks and highways stretched out in diminishing layers. From that height the city looked as if it were made up of small postage stamps of dim colour perforated by roads and the confluence of rivers. He gestured at the view, "When you live on the twenty-third floor you get into the habit of looking down. A man who looks down on the world is sure to fall. Anyway, I'm planning to move to a ground floor apartment as soon as I'm well."

Virginie refused to be sidetracked by his whimsy. "Do you believe Donna was a stigmatic?" she insisted.

Daniel took a long time to answer, so long she thought he'd fallen asleep, but finally he turned to face her again. "No. Briefly. Not now, not anymore. I'm not literal-minded enough."

Virginie knew exactly what he meant, the word he used perfectly summed up the impediment to her own belief. The problem with hysteria, with the psychosomatic disorder, she thought, is that unless you're sufficiently *literal-minded*, metaphors can't help you. She tried to explain her thoughts to Daniel but found herself stumbling over phrases and mispronouncing medical terms. "For me, the psychological explanation simply wasn't enough," she told him in the end. "I don't know why I believed or failed to believe. It would help to know." He, quite rightly, ignored this invitation to speculate on the limits of her faithfulness and they finished their tea in silence.

The room was almost dark, one half of Daniel's face sunk in shadows. When she asked if he'd a clearer idea as to what happened now that he was recovering, he shrugged impatiently as if the question were no longer relevant. "I'm trying to forgive myself—isn't that how psychologists put it—for not being able to believe in the impossible.

"Molly used to say I was the most faithful man she knew, but that's not true, or at least no longer so. Put it like this: when you're in love, it's as if a wound has opened in you. You know you love because you're content to be wounded by her presence, even by her absence. That's how it was with me and God. Now I want nothing so much as a healthy body again, and to hell with the soul."

His words moved her and she began to cry. She wasn't crying for Daniel or for Molly, she wasn't even crying for herself, but for all of them, the sum of their pain larger than each constituent part. She cried for some time, loudly, messily, but without shame, and when she finished it was as if she had poured herself out from a great height into the river below. What was left of her was empty and clear, resonant with each deep breath she took.

"*Hush*," he said, patting her back. They stayed that way for some time.

After a while she told him about the manuscript Molly concocted from the bones of his research, her cunning inventions and sly half-truths, the stories she told about poor Bella-Marie Lambe, and the "journal" that had sprung fully formed from her Zeusian brow.

"Besides your research notes, Molly left me a sheaf of typewritten pages, signed and addressed to *Virginie Waters, my Gentle Reader*." Daniel began to laugh, shallow laughter because of the pain of taking a breath, but no less genuine for that.

"Do you care?" he asked, "I don't. At least someone had

fun with that muddle." Then he asked her to tell him about Molly's death again. How she had been found and if Virginie thought she'd suffered pain. The subject of physical pain was very real to him. Virginie realized he was the kind of patient who remembers pain after it has passed. For him, pain was the wound that forced him open to the world, made him capable of speculating about love and faith to a stranger. She described how she'd found Molly sprawled on the kitchen floor, her arms outstretched.

"And her hands?" he wanted to know. She thought at first he was hinting at what Fisher told her of the burn marks on Molly's palms, but he only wanted to know what she'd been doing when she died.

"Nothing," she said, "her hands were empty."

He repeated the word *empty* on a note of satisfaction, then began to tell a rambling story about his visit to St. Peter's Church in Rome where he'd seen Michelangelo's *Pietà*. The story seemed unrelated to their conversation and she realized he was over-tired. She helped him from his chair, a physical ease between them now, and settled him on the sofa, closing the blinds against the thickening sky. Virginie sat beside him for a long time, talking in a low voice while he fell asleep, half-mumbled questions still forming on his lips, his hand relaxing suddenly in hers.

"You're asleep, you can't hear me now but that's no reason I shouldn't answer. You wanted to know what I thought when I saw Molly dead on her kitchen floor? I thought, *yes*. Yes. I've wondered long and hard about that word and what it implied—affirmation, acceptance, the nervous system's defense at the shock of discovery, or the perverse satisfaction of having one's fears prove grounded. All of these things but more than any one of them, it was simply the continuation of a train of thought that had begun the previous evening when it occurred to me, quite suddenly, that Molly, for all her interest in the dreary details of my life, had never, not once, come up with a single declarative sentence concerning her relationship with my father.

"Did she love him, I wondered, my hands hovering above a sink full of dishes, and although the question had been a long time forming, it demanded an immediate reply so that it was all I could do not to dry my hands on my jeans and sprint barefoot across the trim patch of grass between our houses. I could already imagine myself rapping on the kitchen window, her startled face as she opened the door resolving into a smile of pleasure as she welcomed me. Sit down, she would have said, I'll just switch on the kettle.

"What stopped me was the usual *deus ex machina*, this time in the guise of the Jonarson's Combine that had slipped a clutch and rolled over the ankle of the elder Jonarson. Nurse Freed from the emergency room said that he was in considerable pain, and, knowing Henry Jonarson's intolerance for institutional decorum, I promised I would be right over. Now I think that if I had gone to Molly's instead I might have been in time to save her. Or join her, suggested Fisher, when I put it to him, a little hysterically. But that wasn't all Fisher said.

"It was a cold afternoon with the sulfurous smell of early snow in the air when we buried Molly, and most of the funeral-goers hurried from the cemetery to the Church Hall as soon as was proper. I found myself walking beside Fisher, who had known Molly since he came to the district as a Baby Cop. His expression, not mine. He seemed surprised and approving that I had recovered my equanimity, if not yet my colour, and we spoke for some minutes of his admiration for her humour. I believe the expression *salt of the earth* was used, but I knew he had something on his mind and was simply obeying the proprieties.

"You knew Miss Rhutabaga fairly well, he finally began, I mean her every day habits and so forth? I said I knew of some of her comings and goings, as she did mine, but my work at the hospital kept me away for most of the day and neither of us were in the habit of spying on the other. No, no, he said, that's not what I mean. Do you know, for instance, why she wore gloves when she was at home in the evenings?

"I can't explain the unease his words inspired in me. The cold air entered the layers of my jacket and sweater and thinned my blood. I remembered all the times I'd seen her walking across the lawn between our houses, her airy wave in my direction. She'd been wearing gardening gloves then as, at other times, she had worn rubber washing-up gloves, short, white church-going gloves, and a succession of fur-lined winter mittens. I mumbled something about arthritis but Fisher was having none of that.

"Because it looked as if she'd burnt her palm—palms, he

said, underside of each hand there was a small, round blister, about the size of a dime. Coroner said something about burns, which is why I ask.

"He didn't meet my gaze as I replied that yes, I believe Molly *had* burnt herself one day last week while heating up the wax for the furniture polish. He said good-bye briskly but kindly and hurried off, no doubt to close his file with this last confirmation of Miss Rhutabaga's eccentricity. We both knew she would prefer that to any other sort of speculation.

"I'm not interested in questioning Molly's burns, as I've come to think of them. After this last, bloody summer I've decided to take the physical world on faith. Like some pessimistic old Humian philosopher I'm grateful the sun concedes to rise every day, and equally content that it sets.

"I'm often tired but no longer exhausted, often melancholy but never depressed. My life in this small town seems a happy compromise between an unresolved past and an uncertain future. I imagine myself hanging over this place like a plover in a slip-stream, swinging a latch between earth and sky.

"I had a bad couple of weeks after that. I suffered from insomnia and the nights of sleeplessness pooled beneath my eyes in coffee-stained rings. For a time I became obsessed with imagining a slow death under the blunt blades of the secateur. How would it feel, I wondered, in those moments of consciousness when Molly saw Regina come towards her with the shears, when she realized her throat had been slit, that she was dying like an animal on her kitchen floor. Would there have been time for her life to unwind before her shocked eyes?

"I knew a little about her life—what she'd told me about growing up on this small-holding, her brief marriage and the return to her childhood home where she was to live for the next fifty-three years, interrupted only by her trips North and her brief love affair with my father. Although my religious life these days is entirely non-figurative, I've had the dubious advantage of a Catholic girlhood and, when especially exhausted, have wondered about their reunion. My father wasn't a demonstrative man, but even he, I couldn't help thinking, would welcome her arrival in any heavenly mansion with open arms.

"Well, you can see to what kind of state I'd allowed myself to descend. My dreams were full of dying animals and cut flowers and I developed a tenacious form of eczema on my arms and chest and the skin of my throat.

"What I was suffering from, I finally realized, was grief. Not only, or even mostly, for Molly Rhutabaga whom I had, in my indecisive way, loved, but for the man I could no longer reach because of her death. As long as Molly was alive, I knew there was a way back to my father, some pathway to his mind and heart. She was the repository of his memory and when she died, all possible connection with him died also. In those first weeks I turned the few things she'd told me about him over and over in my mind as I lay in an increasingly sleepless bed, until words unhinged from meaning and the horizon creaked open to release the dawn. I had never cried for my father—neither for his absence nor his death—and I didn't cry now. Instead all tears dried in me and I rattled as I walked.

"If you were awake you'd tell me I was being melodramatic. Such a capacity has never been allowed full rein in my life, but I've always suspected it lurked in the background, threatening to break the bonds of reticence and good breeding. My maternal grandmother was a woman of copious emotion and floating chiffon. As if in partial mourning for her life she went about dressed in pale lilac and a good brooch. She smelled of the parma violets in which her clothes had been folded, and worried at her rosary. I blame her for my tendency to a slight, if concealed hysteria, as well as my dislike of all such breaches of taste. Perhaps that's why I enjoyed Molly's company. She was in all things, deeply, pervasively ironic, and set no store by sentiment.

"I remember coming on her one day in early spring crouched behind the house, burning a pile of yellowing papers. Oh, birthday cards, love-letters, old recipes, she told me, I've no desire to leave a paper trail when I go. Of course that could hardly be true, otherwise she wouldn't have left me her notes and your research, Daniel.

"I began to see that my next step must be to contact you. I was curious as to why you gave her your interviews and transcripts, the work notes you spent so much time collecting and revising. And one more thing. I wanted to see you again, because the journalist I'd spoken to didn't coincide with that other man, the one Molly described, that reader of signs and wonders.

"It's Easter again, one year later. To an impartial observer, little has changed. I get up in the morning, go to work at the hospital, come home exhausted, read a while, take a short walk if the weather permits, then to sleep and begin again. The Rhutabaga homestead was auctioned at a good price and the present owners are happy to allow me to remain as their tenant. Annex has settled into its habitual winter isolation, few people leave and fewer still stay. Nothing of last summer's extraordinary cargo remains. In the little grotto the statue of the Madonna remains where it has fallen after it was pulled down by casual vandals. The Desjardins girl is doing well at school and, to my relief, shows no signs of indecorous bleeding, despite it being the day before Easter.

"In the Catholic church, the purple shroud has been draped over the wooden carving of the crucified Christ in readiness for His Ascension, but few of us, with the possible exception of Father Ricci's mother, expect any visible signs of His resurrection this year. It's as if the final blood-bath in Molly's kitchen purged us all, made us wary of the body's excesses.

"Unlike what preceded it, Molly's death was explicable if scandalous, and, with Regina Arnott diagnosed and locked up in the asylum at Selkirk, there is little to be gained from further speculation. So we have returned to being the small, rather nasty market town of our former days. Since the majority of us are so emphatically in favour of moderation and clean living, I don't think there will be any more blood miracles.

"Regina didn't stand trial for Molly's murder since she was obviously undergoing a psychotic episode at the time of her arrest. Fisher told me she mumbled something about 'the devil in her eyes' when asked why she killed Molly, but was no more forthcoming later. I have never been to see her, I want to believe in her blood-guilt as I never did in Donna's. I hear from a colleague at Selkirk that she has settled into the routine of the place, an untroubled, quiet woman, he says, who wakes herself only to sleep, which she does for marathon lengths of time. She shows no signs of remorse and less of violence, and her religious inclinations have almost vanished, although she does, from time to time, count the beads randomly and without enthusiasm.

"That's everyone accounted for, except me.

"For some time now I've been—well, melancholy is too gentle a word, depression sounds clinical, and unhappiness requires an effort. Call it sadness then, the kind that burrows beneath the skin, making the eyes turn black, the milk turn sour, the windows cloud even in direct sunlight. Not the kind of pain that once tore me into jigsaw pieces, but the kind that settles, reaching its own level in the body. Everything seems motiveless: the sight of the houses in their neat rows, the sad colours of the clapboard, the way the farms encroach on the landscape, the land's failure to escape.

"In my clinic the mothers stand in rows, their hips ajar, roosting children. The drunk late at night on Main, his salty eyes, his stubbed-out mouth, tries with exaggerated caution to balance the sidewalk. The teenagers outside the poolhall, cigarettes gripped between experimental fingers seem as mournful as the patients outside the Care Home, in their hand-me-down coats and gloves. Even the coffee in my mouth these days is like baggy corduroy.

"Perhaps it's a seasonal thing, ice rotting and the rivers breaking up. Beneath the soiled snow we find all the things we've forgotten over the long winter, old letters and bird-prints and clocks still on daylight saving time. And more disreputable things, dog shit and burnt-out resolutions, the year cracking at its fault-line.

"In this last year I've come to think of sadness as a piece of tulle that catches at the barbed wire of memory. Perhaps it's a matter of light—too little or too much, the harsh light of early thaw when we're exposed, the trees unleaved, the sun directly overhead. Perhaps I'm like the ailing physician of legend who tried to diagnose his own condition. I too am trying to cure myself with some version of a more palatable truth.

"You look so peaceful asleep. Didn't Molly say something like that once? At first I thought I could excise memory with a knife, cut out my sadness by confessing, as we used to do in the convent when I was twelve. But now I'm absorbed by the story. I need to know what happens next.

"Over the course of the month after Molly's niece gave me the cardboard box, I read and re-read the strange stories catalogued in your files and Molly's imagination. At first I was intrigued by your conscientious plotting and unruly insights. It was a strange experience to read my own interview. The words I spoke so casually seem mannered in transcription. It was less surprising to learn that you found me aloof, since I'd not welcomed your inquiry in the first place and was decidedly uncomfortable in my role as medical authority in charge of whatever was preying on that poor child's mind.

"Despite my resistance to your methods, I was interested in your need to understand blood miracles through observation, although I was less susceptible to Molly's wild foray into the fourteenth century in search of Bella-Marie Lambe and her scattered wits. In fact, her appropriation of that poor woman's story irritated me out of all proportion until I realized that what she'd done to Bella-Marie she had also done to me.

"I don't keep a journal, have never felt the need to exalt my life to the level of prose. In any case, I've neither the time nor the habit of introspection necessary to sustain a life in writing. Of course I knew Molly was a writer and had read her book on northern rivers with great enjoyment but I never suspected her of the kind of fabrication she was to display. Quite simply, she looted the circumstances of my life and reinvented me as a character named Virginie.

"I was angry with Molly over the manner in which she chose to use my confidences. In fact, I hated reading her invented journal of that irritating Virginie Waters with her martyr complex and her fondness for pain of a metaphysical nature. And, not surprisingly, when you consider my antipathy, I recognized little of myself in the pages of her journal.

"I was interviewed on the radio once, about a rural clinic I opened in the Eastern Townships of Québec, and when I listened to a broadcast of the programme could find no resonance between the voice I knew as my own and the high-pitched, mechanical facsimile on the airwaves. It was the same with the character Molly had created out of the bones and gristle of our late-night conversations.

"*Virginie*—even saying that name makes me uneasy. I imagine the woman Molly described. Thin, somewhat peppery, and suffering from chronic bad circulation. I imagine her cold hands, cold feet, the sharp, thin pinch of her nose. She has a haggard, attractive face, until she smiles, and then it is all Pagliacci disjunction. I think she knows this, for she never smiles, but waves a hand briskly. When not in her hospital whites, she wears muted colours, and in the evenings, often wraps herself in a voluminous shawl with long fringes. Her voice is harsh in timbre, like burnt coffee. When tired she props her head up with a couple of pronged fingers. One is conscious of gravity when around her, and the attraction of the earth's magnetic field. She is not who I am. She is not, has never been, me.

"But Molly's dead and death changes things. After a time I stopped feeling angry at her indiscretions and inventions and simply missed her. I was even a little flattered that she found such absorption in my life. I began to think about truth and falsehood, the whole complicated, sorry mess of this past summer and how nothing has been resolved so much as exhausted.

"Take Donna, for instance. I'm convinced the child was truthful in what she knew. Yet her body's equivocation was so evidently a falsehood. No, I don't mean that she tricked us, not little Donna Desjardins, not even her considerably less malleable mother, but that conniving, demanding God.

"As for Molly, her great contradiction was that she was obsessed with uncovering everyone else's story, at the same time keeping us away from Donna's. We all in our different ways—you through your interviews, Father Ricci, myself—tried valiantly to believe or disbelieve. Massimo avoided the religious significance of the stigmata while I welcomed the psychological. Where we both failed was in believing too quickly. Or believing that knowledge would be enough. Or imagining that information could provide a cure.

"Only Molly remained silent on the subject, invested somehow in keeping us away from Donna even as we strained to reach her. All that talk of mystery and misdirection! No, it was only a muddle and both my professional duty and my personal inclinations urge me to distrust. I don't understand your awe in the face of the inexplicable, neither can I sympathize with Molly's need to search out its cause. It's enough for me to know that such things have, for the moment, ended.

"If there were an alternative, I'd be happy to end this attempt at confession. But having once stepped in blood, I am so far up to my elbows, as a famous king once said, that to go back is as bad as going on. No, I'm determined to see this thing through, and to try to make sense of what happened I'm obliged to find my own place in this story.

"It's not easy for me to confess. I'm what Molly's called an unrequited reader, and I write frequent letters. But it's not at all the same thing as this patient unreeling of the story. Besides, how can I tell what happens when I already know what's happened? I mean, having once told you of Molly's bloody death, how can anything I say about her not—you should excuse the expression—*pale* in comparison?

"I would like, for example, to tell you about the last time I saw her alive, but since I had no idea it would be *the last time*, the visit had no particular significance for me. Yet afterwards, when I discovered her body on the kitchen floor, I returned to that last visit, fingering it in my memory. Sometimes I'm reminded of the cheap thrillers and detective novels I read during my internship, every sideways glance or dropped glove a clue, every clue a detour.

"I'd read those paperbacks during my nights on duty at the training hospital because they were predictable in their wide swings of misfortune. Something occurs, a little out of sequence to be sure, and everything that follows is an attempt to find the hidden order in a story disrupted by death or some other contrivance. In the dim hospital corridors of that time and place, such insistence on parabolic cause and effect was comforting.

"In those books the mystery was always subtle, fraught with coincidence, and ultimately soluble, usually by an exquisitely suited detective with a refined taste in Eighteenth-century snuff boxes. Or a hard drinking, woman-hating private eye with a holster in his side seam, a fifth of bourbon in his hip flask, and a grudge against the world. Nothing could be further from this room.

"The last time I saw Molly she was stooped over her nasturtiums plucking the shallow, round leaves for a late summer salad. The sun was setting behind a clump of old maples, the golden light seeming to catch and kindle their drifting leaves. I thought of God for some reason, or faith at least, perhaps because of the transparency of her skin at that moment, the way I could almost see the blood pulsing at the blue confluence of veins at her wrist and temples.

"I saw a picture of Molly once when she was a young girl. She showed it to me, choosing it carelessly from a box of old photographs. She was standing in that same garden and the surface of the old black-and-white glossy was thick with thumb-prints. She was pretty then, with a mobility of feature that characterized her even in old age. It was as if a smile, a moment of surprise, entirely dispelled her expression of skeptical good temper.

"Molly was not at all one of those old women you see whose character has solidified into flint. She was all shrug and movement, angles of restlessness and shifts of light. That last time she smiled a quick greeting, asking me to hold her basket steady while she snipped at the leaves. Franklin was barking for his supper and she abbreviated her task so as to hurry inside and attend to him.

"I don't know why Molly's death has thrown me into such a jagged depression. Why I wake up nights, my heart—*writhing*—there is no other word for it. I loved my mother consciously, conscientiously, and when she died I mourned for her, I still do. As for my father, I hardly knew him.

"But I'm repeating myself, perhaps because I've so long avoided thinking about Molly's final wish for me. Although she lived for most of her life alone—despite the long-standing affair with my father, she never even contemplated sharing her home with a man again—nothing would have pleased her so much as a romance between you and me, Daniel.

"She talked of you often, your sensitivity, your loneliness. Perhaps in her reckoning I was also lonely. She'd reached that age where the risks she'd been willing to take in her own life were judged too demanding for others, and I was the recipient of her gentle, persistent concern. As for myself, I was *old enough and ugly enough* as my mother would have said, not to imagine that one romance would end happily where so many others had not. And I was not the least attracted to you, Daniel. Any fool could see that you were deathly ill. Or at least believed yourself so.

"It's the night before Easter. This is not a tragedy, just a story about who has continued to bleed and whose bleeding has been staunched. I fall somewhere in between. I'm glad because if there's one thing I've learned it's that a certain amount of bloodshed is necessary to sustain life.

"I will never again bleed as much as I have in these last years, but then, the life expectancy of an emotional hemophiliac is not what it should be. In another year I'll have completed my contract, I'll be free to leave Annex. Until then I'm happy to live in the cabin, and on late spring evenings I sit at my window.

"From the corner of my eye I see the figure of a woman passing across the yard. She carries a bale of twine, or a trowel, or a hitching post. When she sees me she smiles and shifts her load so she can wave. With one neatly gloved hand she waves, *goodbye.*" ꚛ

Acknowledgements

Warm thanks to Aritha van Herk for her generously ungentle readings, for being my guide, philosopher, and friend.

And to Nicole Markotić, *cette amie—cette parente que l'on se fait soi-même.*

I want to thank the Manitoba Arts Council for time and St. John's College, Manitoba, for a place.

The following people have generously influenced, encouraged, and refined my ideas and writing: David Arnason, Robert Budde, Dennis Cooley, Catherine Hunter, Cynthia Jordan, Robert Kroetsch, Mark Libin, Suzette Mayr, Dawne McCance, Pat Sanders, Beryl Walsh, Rudy Wiebe, and David Williams. And, as always, my lovely family.

Méira Cook

Méira Cook was born and raised in Johannesburg, South Africa. In 1991, at the age of 26, she immigrated to Canada. She has worked as an arts reviewer, lecturer, editor, and creative writing instructor. An accomplished poet, Méira Cook has several collections to her credit including the recent *Toward a Catalogue of Falling* and *A Fine Grammar of Bones*. Her prose and poems have appeared in *West Coast Line, Due West, Prairie Fire,* and *Canadian Fiction Magazine*. For many years Méira Cook lived and worked in Winnipeg, Manitoba.